HELLION

MICHELLE MARTINEZ

DISCLAIMER:

This book touches on very sensitive topics that some people may not find suitable. Examples being: murder, suicide, and rape. Reader discretion is advised.

This book is a work of fiction. Any reference to historical events, places, real people, or real places are used fictitiously. Other names, characters, places, and events are products of the author's imagination, and any resemblance to actual events, places, or persons, living or dead, is entirely coincidental.

Cover Design completed by Michelle Martinez with Canva Pro and Infinity Software

Copyright © 2020 Michelle Martinez

ISBN: 978-1-7363249-1-2

First Edition

This book would not exist without the love, support, and guidance of my other half, Emmanuel. I owe him more than I could ever repay.

This book is dedicated to my best friend, Shevelle. She lets me rope her in on some crazy adventures and this book wouldn't be in your hands without her help.

A veil of death that follows wherever he goes.

Those pale blue eyes...that sinister grin.

How far would he be willing to go for his beliefs?

Saving the innocent, punishing the wicked.

He would be the judge,

The jury,

And their executioner...

CHAPTER ONE

Andy Marshall lived in Edgeway, a bustling city full of people he couldn't have cared less about. He wasn't exactly pleased with how his life had turned out; in fact, he could not remember a time before he lived in the city. He hardly remembered his parents, and the five years before he moved to Edgeway were a complete blur to him. Whether this was because of his brief, yet violent, drug addiction or the head wound he received in a traumatic car accident, he was unsure. Andy grew up in Glenwood, a small town in the middle of nowhere, before moving to Edgeway. He was an only child, but, as social as he was, he was never alone. Wanda and Mike Marshall, Andy's parents, owned the town hardware shop. Glenwood was a quiet town until people started dying. The deaths would mess with the heads of the youth, and, eventually, lives would drastically change. Andy ended up flunking his junior year and dropping out before senior year even began. He felt as if this town had a veil of death placed upon it, and he needed to leave. So, with 100 dollars in his pocket and a bag of clothes, Andy took a one-way bus ticket out of town. That choice would end up bringing Andy into a downward spiral.

Andy discovered that starting over was not the easiest thing to do, especially knowing no one. Andy ended up with the wrong crowd, diving into drugs to find meaning in his life. One night, drugged out of his mind, he got behind the wheel of a car. He woke up three weeks later in a hospital in Edgeway. While in that hospital bed, he decided he would get his life back on track. Social workers set him up with a place upon his release, but he needed to support himself. Andy would face the problem of trying to find a job with his record. The only business that would hire someone like him was a fast-food joint. That wasn't exactly what he had planned for his life.

In a chaotic turn of events, he'd somehow come about saving the life of a man named Ralph Smithinson when a building spontaneously collapsed during a fire one dry, hot summer. Overjoyed at the random act of kindness, Ralph gave Andy a job in his company as a thank you, saying over and over that the young lad was his "guardian angel." It had been a reflex; had Andy not pulled Ralph aside when he had, the old man probably would have died. Of course, as time passed, Ralph turned out to be a royal pain in Andy's ass, and he wished he had just let the man die. Ralph was a person who would exaggerate his problems just to make you feel bad about proving him wrong. He would sell his mother if it would be of any profit to him, and he thought the universe revolved around him. He was heartless.

Working for that superficial, pompous man from nine to five for a countless number of years, the twenty-nine-year-old had had enough. It was even safe to say he hated his life with a vicious passion. Between work and the insignificant time Andy had to himself, life was chaotic and stressful. His cubicle-based job in the Smithinson Supply Company was worse than telemarketing (which he had also done before they promoted him). Forced to work with customer support, Andy had the extreme displeasure of dealing with either angry or completely oblivious patrons, day in and day out, as they asked incredibly stupid questions and shouted through their phones at him, as if the product malfunctioning was his fault. People really couldn't seem to get it through their heads that Smithinson Supply did not make the products. They just sold them.

If it wasn't the customers, it was his boss. Ralph Smithinson, aged fifty-two, had the personality of a paper plate. Not even the most profane of curses could describe how horrible this man was. Andy's work performance began slipping, starting last month, because he was growing weary of his mediocre existence. Instead of collecting enough courage to dispose of himself, Andy dedicated what was left of his hopefully brief life to being a complete and total bastard to everybody around him. Suddenly, every day was casual Friday. Andy would just stare emotionless ahead as Ralph chewed him out every morning, merely thinking of what he wanted to say to Mr. Smithinson, instead of having the audacity to speak his mind. However, for whatever reason, on a sunny Monday morning in May, Andy just snapped and finally let it all go.

"Andy, I have a right mind to fire you! Your shirt isn't tucked in! At least I have the decency to come to work looking professional!" Mr. Smithinson barked at him as he rounded the corner, heading for his desk.

Andy stopped dead in his tracks, took a deep, shaky breath, and turned to face his superior. "I certainly hope you would, sir; otherwise, we would all have to deal with that fatty mass you call a stomach hanging out for everyone to see."

Mr. Smithinson turned beet red as he tried to decide if Andy had said that, or if he'd just imagined it. The entire room was dead silent; a few of Andy's co-workers had to choke back giggles and hide behind their cubicles before the storm hit. "You sorry excuse for a human being! Where do you get off insulting me? Are you trying to get fired?" Mr. Smithinson roared, getting right in Andy's face. Oh, but Andy was far from finished. Every bit of hatred he had pushed aside for Ralph had finally broken loose.

"Do you mind, sir? Your breath smells like you licked yourself clean this morning." Andy spoke loudly over his boss's yelling, taking a few steps back to distance himself from Ralph. A woman on her way to the copier glared at the scene wide-eyed and with a faint smile on her face. She wanted to laugh but knew that if she did, it would be her head.

"After all that I've done for you, you treat me this way? I didn't have to promote you; you didn't even deserve it!" Ralph looked like his eyes were about to pop out of his head; he jabbed Andy's chest with his index finger so hard it hurt. Andy grabbed his finger and twisted it back. Ralph squirmed and fidgeted as pain coursed into his eyes and an agonizing grunt escaped his throat. "Assault! I can get you for assault, Marshall! I have the best lawyers in the city in my pock-"

"Oh, come on! Enough!" Andy interrupted him, rolling his hazel eyes. "After all you've done for me? What have you ever done, short of making my life miserable?" He twisted Ralph's finger a little harder as he uttered that last word before continuing. "Constantly, you breathe down my neck, telling me if I shape up, I'll make CEO someday - but you've been saying that for ten years now. I'm still stuck in this stuffy little room with people I can't stand, working for a man who specializes in sitting with his thumb up his ass! I swear to God, I've never seen you lift a finger, not one day in the past decade I've worked here!" Andy shouted, twisting Ralph's finger even harder before letting go as the man screamed out in pain.

"Get out! You broke my finger, you psychotic scum!" Ralph howled, doubled over, holding his right hand as his finger pointed out at an unnatural angle. Andy could admit he hadn't intended to break it, but he was furious. He wasn't going to take it anymore.

As Andy walked away, he turned around and waved his middle finger high in the air. "I'm scum? You're no better than me! If I could go back in time to the day of that fire, I'd leave you there to die!" He stormed out of the room and down the stairs before Ralph could retaliate. He almost wanted to laugh. It felt good getting all of that off his chest. His only problem now was that he didn't have a job and would probably go to jail.

As Andy stepped out of the door and onto the sidewalk, a female voice hailed him, "Andy!"

He shot her a sidelong glance and continued walking. Her name was Jenna, and to be honest, he couldn't stand her. She was a little younger than him and had one of those energetic personalities that most found attractive, but he found it appalling. He believed Jenna was naïve; how could she be so in love with the world and life when the true reality was that things never go the way you want them to? Just as Andy satirically recommended to himself that he change his name to Mr. Cynical, Jenna shouted his name again while running the best that she could in high heels without falling all over herself.

"Slow down! Hey! Come on!" He couldn't believe it - she was laughing. He slowed his pace a little so she could catch up, looking ahead and barely acknowledging her when she came up to his side. "What's your problem, Andy? That was hilarious. You pretty much said what all of us have been thinking all year!" Jenna paused for a moment while flipping her hair out of her face to get a better look at Andy. "He's going to press charges, you know. Already was trying to get someone to call the cops before I left the office. Couldn't get out the words, though. You did a number on him while barely touching him."

"He can shove his charges. He assaulted me first, by all technicalities. Jabbed me in the chest. I think I have a welt." Jenna laughed again, her blonde hair bouncing as she tried to keep in pace with him. Andy hadn't meant that to be funny, but he was sort of mocking Ralph's melodramatic tendencies. Though Andy usually was a fast walker, at the moment, he was going the extra mile in an attempt to ditch her. It was futile, of course; the only way Jenna would ever take a hint was if you spelled it out for her. As cold as he was, Andy never had the heart to be nasty to her. He didn't want to rain on her parade or burst her bubble. Though he envied her for her unexplained happiness,

7

the last thing Andy wanted was for her to be miserable along with him. He just wanted to be alone.

"Where are you headed?" Jenna asked when Andy finally stopped to wait for the "WALK" sign to turn green again. He had half a mind to just walk right out into the oncoming traffic. A light, warm breeze ruffled his sandy brown hair as he leaned against the pole.

"Charlie's. Where else?" he muttered, as if she should have known. Charlie's was a bar a few blocks down from where he worked - well, used to work. It was pretty sad; even people who had never been to Charlie's before knew Andy by name.

Jenna looked at him, downtrodden and sad. "Oh Andy, that's the last place you should go. How many drinks do you have on average? You're going to kill yourself." She scanned him with blue eyes, waiting for a response. If only she knew how much he wished that very thing lately. Andy was certain it'd break her heart. He wasn't sure, but he had a hunch that Jenna might have a thing for him. He hadn't the slightest idea why. She could do so much better; he was sure of that.

Andy ran his fingers through his hair and rubbed his stubble before letting his arm fall back down to his side. "Shouldn't you be at work, or did you quit, too? Break any of his other fingers by chance?"

She smirked and chuckled, shaking her head. "You always avoid answering things like that. I had today off, remember? I came in to give Smithinson that report and then head back home."

The "WALK" sign finally turned green, and they hurried across the street because it had a habit of turning red about ten seconds afterward. Andy was certain the street lights in Edgeway had a secret agenda to kill as many people as they could. "Well then, shouldn't you be heading back home?" Andy was laying it on pretty thick, but Jenna wasn't getting the fact he wanted to be alone.

"Not with an emotionally distressed friend on my hands, I'm not," she replied, hooking his arm with her elbow. She did that a lot, and it irritated him. Any other man would kill to have Jenna hold him by the arm, but not him. Andy could admit she was a very gorgeous girl, but his life was a mess, and he really couldn't see dragging someone else into it. He vaguely remembered a time when he wouldn't have minded her company, but those days were long gone.

"Charlie's isn't the best environment for a girl like you. Lots of pigs." He slipped his arm away and pushed his hands into his pockets while continuing onward.

Jenna almost sent him over the edge with what she did next - she slid her hand into his pocket and laced her fingers between his. "Then let's not go to Charlie's..."

He felt incredibly uncomfortable but could neither take his hand out of his pocket nor squirm his way out of her grip. Andy didn't exactly have much room in his pockets. He figured Jenna must have very tiny hands, which would allow her to hold his hand like she was. He was at her mercy and felt even more awkward asking her to let go, so he lied a bit. "You're, uh, kind of hurting my finger. I slammed it in the door this morning."

As he expected, Jenna apologized, her face flushed, and she immediately withdrew her hand. He felt bad that he had lied to her and, even worse, embarrassed her. Andy hated her for being one of his very few soft spots, and when she changed the subject, it overjoyed him. "So, where else would you want to go? Grab a bite to eat, maybe?"

He exhaled and spoke, "Nah, I just want to go see Charlie." *Oh, my... just go away, please...*

There was a pause before she responded. "Oh..." Jenna looked away almost immediately. For some bizarre reason, Andy wondered if she could read his thoughts. "Well... if you want to take me up on that offer, you know my cell number, right?"

"Yup," he said, lying again and hating himself even more for it. Andy was glad that Charlie's was just at the end of the next street. He wanted to sprint the rest of the way, just to get away from Jenna before being even more of an ass to her. "You'll probably see me around, most likely on the news. Ralph will make a big deal out of this, I'm sure," he said, not trying to be funny but meriting a laugh from Jenna all the same. They had reached Charlie's at last.

"Call me, okay? Here - just in case you forget my number." She handed him one of her business cards. Jenna floored him sometimes. Whether or not she was aware of it, she always managed to eliminate all of Andy's possible ways to avoid her. They said their goodbyes, and he watched Jenna walk away until he couldn't see her anymore before heading into Charlie's.

CHAPTER TWO

It was dimly lit inside Charlie's, as usual, but it was relatively empty. The normal crowd hadn't shown up since it was so early in the day. Charlie - a big, Australian, muscular man who always wore his hair back in a ponytail - was behind the bar, cleaning a glass when Andy walked in. Although Andy was a rather heavy drinker, Charlie was surprised to see him. "Andy! What the hell are you doing here so early? It's not even noon," he said in an accent smoother than silk, as he set the glass down with a grin.

"I quit my job... violently," Andy grumbled, crawling up onto his favorite bar stool.

"Uh-oh, how violently?" Charlie planted his palms on the counter and leaned in to listen.

"Broke Ralph's finger." He couldn't help but smile.

"Jesus, Andy!"

"I didn't mean to! He started it, anyway. Got in my face. I am so sick of his attitude, Charlie. I'm done with him." Andy leaned back and sighed. "Can I get a beer? Any kind is fine, I really don't care anymore."

Charlie reluctantly grabbed a random bottle out of the cooler and set it on the coaster in front of Andy. He sucked in a breath through his teeth and Andy thought, *here it comes, the dad lecture.*

"What do you plan on doing now, Andy? Do you ever think ahead? You know you could go to jail for this, right?"

"They can execute me for all I care," he grunted, twisting the top off his drink and taking a sip.

"I hate it when you talk like that." Charlie flipped on the television in the corner to kill the awkward silence between them. Andy was the closest thing to a brother the bartender had ever had, and though he wouldn't openly say it, Charlie was worried sick about him half the time.

"In any case, Ralph won't do jack shit. I have knowledge of every illegal thing he's taken part in, and he knows it. If he squeals on me, I can take him down with me. Simple as that. I may just turn him in anyways, he doesn't deserve another day as a free man."

Charlie snorted. "I'm sure if you had it your way, you would kill him, wouldn't you?"

13

Andy smirked while cocking his head to one side, pondering for a moment. "I still might."

They shared a good laugh about the whole thing but were interrupted as the door to the bar opened, granting entrance to a man Andy had never seen before. Judging by the look on Charlie's face, Andy was sure he hadn't seen him before either. Tall, lanky (but not in an unattractive way), and well dressed; he waltzed into Charlie's like he owned the place. He didn't even bother to take his sunglasses off. Sporting a black Armani suit, a bright red undershirt, and bouncing jet-black feathered hair, he looked like he had walked straight out of Hollywood. Charlie greeted him without an ounce of intolerance.

"G'day there! Haven't seen your face before, sir. You new in these parts?"

The man tipped his head and smiled widely. A real hot-shot. Andy hated him already. "Actually, yes I am. Here on business, heard this place has great drinks and fantastic buffalo wings."

Charlie gave a hearty laugh. "Well then, you've come to the right place, but the grill ain't on yet."

He gave a nod of understanding and sat right next to Andy. He had the entire bar to sit, and he had to plant right next to him. Andy hated it when people did that, or was it just that Andy hated people? Both were the same in his mind. The man didn't even ask if he could sit down there or if the seat was free. *What a pompous bastard*, Andy thought.

The gentleman turned to Andy, sunglasses still on, perfect white smile staring him dead in the face, and extended his hand to him. "Name's Sid Hellion. Who, if I may ask, are you?"

Andy gave him a hostile look before taking Sid's hand and shaking it out of respect for Charlie. "Andy." He didn't feel inclined to announce his full name, like a certain grinning jackass next to him.

"Nice to meet you, Andy. I assume you're Charlie, then?"

The Australian nodded his head with a wink. Andy couldn't believe that Charlie would like Sid, when he was already annoyed to no end with the newcomer.

"Good, good," said Sid. "Say, Andy, you kinda look like all Hell broke loose on you today."

Charlie laughed, "You dunno the half of it, mate. Let me go get the kitchen opened up so you can get some wings. I will be right back."

He left Andy alone with Sid, which may have not been the smartest thing in the world, considering how Andy was feeling. Andy chose to grin and bear it. He hoped Sid wouldn't become a regular. If he did, he would have nowhere to go to get away from it all. "Yeah, it kinda did," Andy said flatly, taking a long drink from his beer. Sid Hellion, what kind of name was that? He was probably a rock-star wannabe. He definitely looked the part, at least.

"It's a shame you're having such a bad day so early on. Anything you'd like to talk about?" Sid asked, leaning back and turning towards Andy.

"You're real outgoing, aren't you? I don't need another friend, Sid. Don't mean to burst your bubble."

To further his irritation, Sid just laughed at him and lowered his sunglasses with one finger. He looked like he'd been practicing the move all morning, but Andy couldn't comment further on it because he was suddenly distracted by Sid's eyes. They were a terrifyingly pale shade of blue. He almost looked insane with how much his pupils stood out. "What, like you don't want to burst Jenna's bubble?"

The seductive tone in Sid's voice, and the fact he knew about Jenna, unsettled Andy. "How the hell do you know her?" he demanded.

Sid drew in closer to him and wiggled his fingers, blue eyes wide and manic-looking, as they peeked over the rim of his glasses. "I'm psychic."

Andy raised a brow. This guy was a lunatic, a stalker, or something. He couldn't even come up with something hostile or satirical to say to that. Andy was speechless. In the background, a meteorologist rattled off the daily forecast, but the room was otherwise silent. Sid continued to stare at Andy with his manic eyes for another moment or two before bursting into a fit of laughter that would have put a hyena to shame. He literally had the laugh of a mad scientist. Was this guy for real?

"I'm just screwing with you, man; I saw you walking with her on the way here. I'm very good at reading people. I could tell you were forcing yourself to be nice to her."

Even though it was the truth, it bothered Andy. Andy tripped over his words, which never happened. "I wasn't forcing myself... I just..."

Sid put his hand up and shook his head at Andy. "Ah-ah-ah, don't worry. Your secret is safe with me. The only thing I can't figure out about you is why you wouldn't accept the affection of that," he pressed his thumb, middle, and index finger together and kissed their tips, "magnificent woman."

Still holding onto the thought that Sid was stalking him, Andy gave into the small talk. "Five minutes alone with her and you'd see why, I'm sure." Immediately, he wished he hadn't said it that way because Sid struck him as the kind of guy who would twist his words and turn it into something dirty.

"Five minutes alone with her and I'd see something." He waggled his eyebrows like Groucho Marx and carved a wicked smile into his face.

Seething, Andy turned away from Sid. "Don't talk about her like that."

"Oh-ho-ho! Hit a nerve? You care about her, don't you?"

Charlie emerged from the back room, wiping his hands on a rag. He had just rescued Sid from a punch in the face because Andy didn't want to start a fight in front of him. Fist shaking, he left it at his side. Andy didn't know how Sid had so much knowledge about Jenna and himself, but he was certain that it had nothing to do with the fact that Sid paid close attention to detail. Nobody could find out that much just by watching a conversation.

"Andy, you look a bit miffed. Everything alright?" Charlie asked without looking at him, tossing the rag aside.

"It's my fault, Charlie. I tried to make pleasant conversation about his little lady friend and crossed the line," Sid offered, but didn't show a hint of regret in his voice.

"Who? Jenna?" Charlie stated, turning towards the men. Charlie was one of the few people who Andy had opened up to about anything, so he knew a bit about Jenna.

"Can we just shut up about her already? Let me relax? Please?" Andy had never been more annoyed in his life.

"Well, since you used the p-word..." Sid began. Charlie followed with a loud bit of laughter.

That was it for him. Andy chugged the rest of his beer and slammed the bottle on the counter along with a five and told Charlie to keep the change. He slid off his barstool and headed towards the door. Charlie called after him with apologies, but Andy wasn't listening. The only place he had left to go was home. He hated his apartment building, but at least Sid wasn't there.

CHAPTER THREE

Andy trudged down the sidewalk, lost in thought, brooding over everything he had done that morning. Had it been worth it? He couldn't help but chuckle at the memory of the face that Ralph made when he broke his finger, but beyond that, he gained no other satisfaction. He had vented, spoken his mind. He was still miserable, if not worse off. A homeless man sat against a building on the corner, a can of change at his feet. Andy was half inclined to drop a few bucks in, but went on to "accidentally" kick it halfway across the street, instead. Change and singles scattered around as the man cursed and howled at him, scrambling to get his money back, and Andy felt nothing short of self-loathing for what he'd just done.

"You're a mess," Sid's voice came from… his mind? That was absolutely insane. Andy looked around him, then behind him. He lingered only for a moment before turning around again, to find Sid staring at him with his cold, blue eyes. Naturally, Andy flinched.

"Didja hear me? You're a mess. Look what you did to that poor slob over there!" He spoke in a motherly tone, shaking his index finger at him. Andy pushed past him and continued walking.

"He'll probably just use it to buy booze and drugs anyways," Andy muttered.

"What else should he use it for? He's homeless," Sid replied, catching up with Andy. He smirked at him. "You've got a home, bank account, *and* had a job, and you use your money on all of that, too."

Sid had a point. Andy really hated him for it. "Shut up. How do you know I lost my job?"

"Charlie told me before I left. I personally would have pissed my pants laughing if I had seen what you did to your boss. He is a cheat; I'll give you that. I know the guy, a real slime."

Finally, something Andy could agree with Sid on. Andy gave him no response, hoping his silence would drive him away, but it didn't. Sid just kept right on walking beside Andy, all the way to his apartment. If he wasn't so mentally drained, he would have continued walking until Sid finally gave up, but Andy was just too tired to care at this point. "What, are you lost or something? You've been following me forever." They stopped in front of his apartment building. The building was small compared to others in the vicinity. It was also cheap.

"Actually, it's only been a half-hour," Sid stated as he glanced at his watch. Andy reached for the door to his building as Sid continued, "Plus, no place to stay at the moment."

That halted Andy right in his tracks, and he turned back towards Sid, who had a big menacing grin on his face. "Didn't your business give you a hotel room?"

"I said I was here on business, that doesn't mean I work for somebody." Sid chuckled, and he reached for the door to the apartment complex. He wondered if Sid was looking for a recommendation, as he was not from the area, but Andy had never stayed in a hotel nearby. Sid opened the door for Andy and responded, "After you."

"I know of a few hotels in the area. I could get you a phone book or something." Andy quickly passed Sid and headed straight up the stairs, instead of waiting for the elevator that worked when it wanted. There was really no getting rid of this guy, Andy figured out as he hastened his pace up the stairs, Sid close behind. He was like a lost puppy, following him around, except Andy had never felt the urge to strangle a puppy like he wanted to do to Sid.

"Actually, I'd like it if I could stay with you for a while, old buddy. You need help, a friend, someone to help you get your life back on track. Look at you! You're miserable, and I hate to use the word but,"

21

Sid paused as Andy glanced back, "pathetic. I kinda like you. You interest me." Sid began to pant, struggling to keep up with Andy.

When they got to the top flight, Andy spun around and looked at Sid with a mixture of confusion and disgust. Andy's hands went up to stop Sid from coming closer. "Look! I'm not your 'old buddy.' I've never met you in my life."

"Oh, but you have. You just don't remember me, that's all. I remember you, yes I do! You've been in my head a lot lately, as a matter of fact." Sid stared at Andy almost quizzically, steepling his fingers before resting his index fingers against his bottom lip.

Andy stared back at Sid, speechless. He took a moment, mouth hanging open before responding. "You're creeping me out, man," he said at last, shaking his head and turning away. It would be the last thing Andy would ever say to Sid if he had his way. But with Andy, he never had such luck. He walked away quickly towards his apartment door, aiming to slip inside and lock himself within for a few days. Unless Sid had enough time on his hands to camp outside and wait, Andy was sure this bizarre man would be out of his hair by Friday. But Sid caught up with him, putting his long, skinny arm around his shoulders and somewhat leading him into his apartment, laughing all the way. Andy threw Sid's arm off and pushed him into a wall. "Let me spell it out for you. I. WANT. TO. BE. ALONE. Okay? I don't like you. I don't want you to stay with me, and

I don't want you hanging around my bar."

Sid's hair had fallen in front of his eyes, and he was grinning. He looked absolutely insane and terrifying at that moment, with his head lowered like a psychotic hungry wolf as he leaned against the wall. "You're feisty," he chuckled finally, pursing his lips into a little pout and slicking his hair back. "You're also mean. I'm new to this school, Andy; I need a friend. I don't want to have to sit with the outcasts at lunch anymore." Sid spoke in a whiny little kid's voice. Then he started laughing and closed the door behind him.

"Whatever," Andy muttered, walking further into his messy apartment. What is the worst that would happen? Sid kills him? That sounded like heaven. He had given up on driving Sid away; he was too crazy for him. If he wanted to stay, fine. Andy didn't care anymore. Not about life, not about work, not about anything. It had been one of the most stressful days he'd ever been forced to live through, and he hadn't gained a moment's peace. It didn't look as though he would find solace, even at home, with Sid Hellion breathing down his neck.

By Friday, Sid was still staying with Andy. He had put up with the crazy, wide-eyed antics of his new psychotic roommate for almost an entire week, and Andy couldn't help but admit the man was growing on him. Sid had made him laugh the other day, which was rare. In fact, Andy was feeling almost happy. He wasn't looking for a job, and Ralph was still threatening to call the police. Andy threatened Ralph back, providing him with a rebuttal. He could blow the top off of Ralph's whole embezzlement plot and take him down, if he wanted to press charges for the broken finger.

Although Andy was getting along with Sid a little better than before, he felt a little uncomfortable around him. Sid liked to screw around too much. On Tuesday, he crawled in bed with him, putting on his whiny kid voice again, saying that the thunderstorms were scaring him when it wasn't even raining outside. Andy shot through the ceiling then, almost punching Sid in the face because he'd woken Andy out of a dead sleep by huddling into his side like a child. After Andy had shoved Sid off the bed, he merely laughed his crazy laugh and told him he was too homophobic. Andy chucked a pillow at him and said, "That isn't the point, you scared the hell out of me!" To which Sid raised an eyebrow and replied seductively, "Oh, so you don't mind?"

Things like that, paired with the everyday human male immaturity, made up what Andy had to learn to tolerate, and, by the time Friday rolled around, actually began to like. Looking back on everything Sid had done to him that week, Andy couldn't help but laugh.

Andy crawled out of bed and walked past the living room to find Sid was not on the couch, ruling that he was probably awake and possibly hiding somewhere to tackle him as he came into the kitchen or something. But surprisingly, Sid was just calmly sitting at the breakfast table with food all ready and cleaning his nails with one of Andy's knives. As he sat down, Sid adopted a British accent and said, "Good morning, love."

Andy rubbed his eyes and half-yawned, half-laughed. "Cut that out man, it's creepy," he commented, ignoring the fact they were both two grown, single men sitting at the breakfast table in their boxers.

"Oh, you know you love it," he continued in his accent and, with a goofy grin, let the chair fall on all fours and threw the knife in the sink behind him. "I made sausage," he sang, gesturing to the stove.

"Thanks," Andy chuckled, rising to his feet. "You know, Sid, you're all right." He walked over to the frying pan and picked out what he wanted and then went on, "I hated you at first. You really turned it around. I think you're the first real friend I've had in a long time."

"Aw," Sid cooed as Andy took a seat again. "You really like me? I'm charmed." He sounded almost like he was mocking him, but Andy knew by now that is just how Sid talked.

"Yeah, I do. It's a major accomplishment to win me over. Not even Jenna could do it." The mere mentioning of her reminded Andy that he had never called her. It made him feel bad, even though he didn't care - or at least, thought he didn't. "Oh, hey. I've been wondering something lately. You never said anything more about it, but what kind of business are you on that brings you to Edgeway, anyway?"

Sid grinned, "I've been waiting for you to ask me that. I've known you for a long time, Andy. But I never got to know you. You're a really nice guy, you know how to take a joke... it's a shame I have to do this..."

Before Andy could ask, Sid overturned the table in a violent flurry of silverware and food. Bewildered, he kicked the table off him and scrambled on all fours into the living room, shouting obscenities and frantic questions. "Sid! What the fuck, man?! What the hell is the matter with you? What do you have to do?"

He didn't speak. Sid looked vicious. His eyes were alive with something sinister, a terrifying emotion that Andy couldn't place. It was the look a predator gets before it kills its prey. Andy rolled onto his back, trying to scurry away from the furniture, to turn over as Sid advanced on him, bare chest heaving with adrenaline-fueled breaths. Was Sid a hit-man? Did Ralph set this up? Andy didn't even get a chance to ask him, though he was sure Sid wouldn't have given him an answer. He felt Sid's bare foot collide with his jaw, and his body whipped to the side from the impact. Sid kicked him hard. His lip was bleeding. Andy was on his knees, leaning over, holding his face.

"Ralph didn't send me, Andy. I sent me." Sid seemed to read his mind again.

"Why?" Andy spat, trying to stand up. Sid put his foot on the small of his back and leaned down, picking his head up by his hair.

Andy could feel his breath in his ear as

he leaned closer, chuckling in a tone that was low and eerily haunting. "You've been in my head for a long, long time, Andy. I told you that. It took me a long time to find you, but it has all paid off." His voice was raspy and laced with insanity. Andy felt his face smash into the floor, his nose cracking and breaking. Andy screamed and lashed his leg back, clipping Sid in the shoulder with his heel. It was enough to get him off his back. Andy suddenly didn't want to die anymore. He wanted to live. He had a new love for life, he wanted to enjoy what he had now - he didn't want to be miserable anymore. He wasn't about to give up just yet.

Andy rolled, nose gushing blood, and slammed his other heel into Sid's eye about three times before the crazed man got out of kicking range and stood, howling in agony, clutching his left eye socket with both hands. Sid staggered backwards into the kitchen, tripping over the table and cracking the back of his head on the counter. Andy stumbled after him, almost falling over the table, catching himself on the counter with his palm. Andy reached across and grabbed a knife out of the sink, just as Sid planted his foot into his gut and sent him flying back over the table again and into the living room. In a fury of terror and adrenaline, Andy stood to meet Sid as he lunged and thrust the knife deep into Sid's bare stomach. He stopped dead in his tracks, inhaling sharply and gasping in pain. Andy twisted the knife and dragged it through muscle and flesh all the way up to his rib cage before pulling it out and stabbing again, this time aiming for the heart. Pale eyes wide and glassy, Sid fell to the ground. Suddenly, Andy felt faint. Everything went black.

CHAPTER FOUR

Andy heard someone snap their fingers just as he came to. "Sid! Sid, can you hear me?"

The voice belonged to a man. Andy blinked dumbly, staring at the man across the table from him as he came into focus. He was in a stark white room, sitting in a chair with his arms resting on the table in front of him. What had happened after he passed out? How did he get here? The man across the table spoke a second time, tapping the wood surface with his finger.

"Did I lose you there for a moment? Sid, can you hear me?" The man shifted in his seat and began making notations in the notebook in his lap before speaking again. "Notation, subject took twenty-seven seconds to come out."

Who was he talking to? Come out of what? Was Andy in jail or a police station? This didn't look like any police station he had seen before. Wait, did he just call him Sid? Why was he calling him that? Did Sid survive somehow and try to switch them around? His license would prove he is not Sid. "I'm not Sid. I'm Andy. Sid... he's... he's gotta be dead... I think. I stabbed him. He attacked me... and I stabbed him," he replied blankly, trying to piece everything together. What had happened? He began trying to recall the events of last night. Tonight, what time is it?

The man sighed, leaning his elbows against the table. "Do you know my name?"

Andy's eyebrows scrunched together. "No... should I?"

"You should, I've told you before. It's Jack. Sid, my name is Jack. I'm a psychiatrist. We have been meeting for quite some time now, remember?"

Andy was becoming irritated. "My name is not Sid! He is dead! I can prove it! My finger prints are in the system. Run them, and you will see! Or just look at my ID. Where the hell am I, anyway?"

Jack rubbed his hand over his forehead, frustration shown across his face. "Why don't we take a walk?" Andy realized that that was more of a demand than a question. Jack stood up and placed a tape recorder in his pocket. Andy had not seen that sitting on his lap before. Was he hoping for a confession? The notebook, he tucked under his left arm while gesturing with his right for Andy to lead the way out of the room.

Jack followed Andy out of the room before coming beside him and leading him down the bare hallway, talking all the while. Doors lined the hallway. It was eerily quiet, and it seemed too clean for a police station. "You're in Brookhaven Psychiatric Hospital, Sid," he said, gesturing in front of them. "You were admitted here shortly after your conviction..."

Andy cut him off, "Conviction?! What the hell are you going on about?"

Jack placed a hand gently on his shoulder. "Please give me a moment to explain. I will get you all caught up and hopefully on the right track once again. I apologize, as things did not go as planned today. It has been a while since you have slipped when we have discussed the past." Jack paused a moment before continuing. The look in his eyes seemed pained and made it seem like it was difficult to say what was coming next. "Sid, you are a serial killer. You slaughtered ten people and slowly lost your mind with every kill; such was your plea of insanity, and why you came here. I offered to care for you here when I heard of your case. We sat down for an interview, as was your request. You didn't want just anyone to hear your side of the story."

Andy stopped dead in his tracks, attempting to understand what just came out of this man's mouth. His head slowly started to shake back and forth as he realized what this Jack guy just said. Andy turned towards him quickly. "You've got

the wrong person! I'm Andy! Sid is dead!"
Andy repeated, more frantically this time.

Jack stopped and turned to face him.
"Sid, Andy is dead. While under hypnosis,
you have admitted to all your crimes,
including the murder of Andy. You have
tried to take responsibility for a death that
you did not cause as well, but we have
been working through that. Well, we have
been working through everything."

"What?"

Jack sighed and continued walking.
"You were haunted by what you had done
to Andy Marshall. He was the last man
that you killed. He had been one of your
best friends in high school. You murdered
him just a few months ago. You stabbed
him multiple times, after you beat him. It
was the only crime that you committed
that police could pin on you because of all
the evidence left behind in your frenzy..."
Jack's voice faded away as Andy's blood
ran cold.

*"You've been in my head a lot lately, as
a matter of fact..."* Sid quoted himself
spontaneously in Andy's memory. He still
didn't understand what was going on. He
needed answers. This just couldn't be
right. This couldn't be happening. "Jack?"

"Yes?"

"Where is Edgeway? How far are we
from it?" Andy asked.

"Sid, Edgeway doesn't exist as a city. It
was the name of your high school, where
you lived the best years of your life, or so
you told me. Even then, there were
issues."

He felt faint. Andy leaned against the

wall, breaking into a cold sweat. His stomach churned; his heart raced. "Jenna? Charlie? Ralph? Who are they, then?"

"Girlfriend, step-brother, principle," Jack answered, in order. Andy looked at him, forlorn. "Jenna and Charlie call often. You haven't been allowed to have visitors lately. We are still working with you, trying to find the right medications. We promised to get you on the right track, Sid. We just couldn't risk another outburst, like the one that happened with Jenna's last visit. You ended up regressing quite a bit, so we are working to get you back to where you were. You have never told me, outside of hypnosis, what happened with Andy and Jenna, but whatever it was, it has triggered multiple manic episodes. This is what we are facing right now. Discussing Andy's death and what led to it, you don't seem to be able to handle it."

"I'm Andy. I swear it," he sobbed. "Sid and I look nothing alike! How could you confuse us?"

Jack placed a hand on Andy's back and said, "Let's go this way." He led Andy to the end of the hall to a solid, light brown, wooden door. "Give me a moment," Jack said as he reached into his pocket. Andy began to shake, and not because it was cold. He almost felt... scared. Pulling out a key, Jack unlocked the door in front of them and guided Andy inside. "Sid, please do me a favor and look in the mirror."

Andy glanced towards the sink and mirror in the corner of the room, like it was some kind of rabid animal ready to pounce. He didn't want to look. Why did

Jack want him to look?

"Sid, look in the mirror," Jack repeated, sterner this time.

Andy snapped and screamed, "I'm not Sid! I'm Andy! My name is Andy Marshall!"

Jack grabbed his arm and pushed him in front of the mirror. Andy looked away, sobbing frantically, trying to resist Jack as he grabbed his face and forced him to look. He stopped struggling immediately. He pressed both hands upon the sink, holding himself upright to keep from fainting. It wasn't right, something was wrong. Andy wasn't staring at himself - he was staring at Sid. He blinked, so did Sid. He waved his hand, and Sid copied him. He ran his skinny fingers through his hair, which instead of being its sandy tone, was as black as the night. Sid followed his movements. Andy looked into those cold, blue eyes filled with tears, puffy and red, glistening in the artificial light.

Andy was Sid. That entire fight, that whole terrible week, had it really taken place inside his own mind? Sid had aimed to get rid of his remorse. He hadn't expected Andy to win the fight. His personality had split. Andy was trapped - Sid was dead, and Andy was trapped.

He screamed, shouted, kicked, and howled as Jack backed out of the bathroom. His agonized voice seemed to echo throughout the entire hospital, carrying to all within earshot his message:

"I'm **not** Sid! I'm Andy! I'm Andy! **I'M ANDY!**"

CHAPTER FIVE

21 Years Earlier

He sat on the bench, staring into the park, blue eyes glistening in the light. Being only eight years old, it was hard being so alone. Sidney watched as a small group of kids from his class went running past. Not one kid looked his way. Why would they? They ignored him in school when they weren't picking on him. Why would the park be any different? Lost in thought, Sidney was startled when a hand tapped him on his shoulder. Sidney jumped up from the bench and quickly turned.

"Sidney, I'm sorry. I didn't mean to scare you." She smiled at him while smoothing out her dress with one hand.

"Hi, Becca," he said, lowering his head while sitting back down on the bench.

Rebecca walked around to his front and held out one of the plastic bags in her hands, smiling ear to ear. "Sandwich? It is peanut butter and jelly. Strawberry Jelly, which I know is your favorite."

Sidney looked at the bag and then up at her. A small smile appeared on his face as he took the sandwich from her. "Thank you." It amazed him that she knew his favorite jelly, and Sidney was awfully hungry. Rebecca was one of the few kids who had anything to do with him. She was always so nice to him, but it didn't make anything less awkward for him.

By the time Rebecca sat down next to Sidney, he had almost his entire sandwich gone. Rebecca scrunched her eyebrows together as she looked quizzically at him. "Hungry?"

"Sorry," Sidney said as he struggled to talk with a full mouth. He watched as Rebecca opened a second bag containing another sandwich. She smiled at him while taking a bite as Sidney swallowed what he had in his mouth. At that moment, a pit formed in his stomach; the sandwich felt like a rock.

Rebecca set her sandwich down in her lap before turning towards him more. "When was the last time you ate? My mom says eating too fast can cause a stomachache."

Sidney put his head down. This was the first bit of food he had eaten in almost forty-eight hours. He had attempted to go home two nights ago, on Friday, after school had let out. His mother had answered the door and told him to go somewhere else, that she was "entertaining" for the night. He slept on the back stairs that were never used in the apartment building. In the morning when he had woken, the door was locked, and his mom was either passed out, gone somewhere, or dead. It was now Sunday, and he hadn't yet attempted to go back home. Usually when she leaves, she comes home late Sunday night or early Monday morning. In the meantime, he had to fend for himself. He finally decided to open up to Rebecca. "At school on Friday," he said in a hushed tone, head still hanging.

Her eyes widened at his response. There had been whispers throughout the school, teachers speaking between each other about Sidney's clothes or the fact that he smelled. The only time he ever showered was when he went to the after-school program and used the high school showers. He tried to go there a couple times a week, but no matter how much he showered, wearing the same clothes didn't help much. The next thing Sidney knew, Rebecca had him by the hand and was pulling him away from the bench. "Come on! Let's go!"

"Wh-where are we going?" Sidney said, nervously.

"To get some actual food," Rebecca smiled proudly. "I will not let my friend go hungry. Nope! Not on my watch!" She continued to pull him along until they came to a small group of adults. Sidney recognized Mrs. Potter almost immediately. Mrs. Potter worked at the school in the office, where he was sent frequently. "Mom... mom... MOM!" Rebecca shouted to Mrs. Potter before she turned her attention to them. Mrs. Potter opened her mouth to respond, but Rebecca beat her to it. "Can Sidney come over for dinner? He would really like to come over for dinner. Wouldn't you?" Rebecca nudged Sidney in the rib cage.

"Wh-uh-mm..." Sidney stumbled over his words. He had no idea what to say, especially being put on the spot like that.

Mrs. Potter smiled sweetly, "Of course he can, honey. You can even borrow some swim trunks from her brother and go swimming, if you want."

"What time are we heading home, mom?" Rebecca stated plainly, obviously being very impatient.

"Well, it is quarter to four, and the roast should be done about four-thirty. If you want, we can head home now so you and Sidney can get some swim time in. Just make sure your mom knows where you are, Sidney."

Sidney's eyes went wide. How was he supposed to let her know? He didn't even know where she was. Sidney backed away. "I... ugh... my mom..."

Mrs. Potter's face twisted when everything came together. "It's alright, dear," she said, reaching out her hand to Sidney. "Let's just get you back to our place, and we can worry about that later, alright?"

Sidney gave a small smile. It was the few unspoken moments like this that made him realize that there was good in this world.

Thirty minutes and a short drive later, Sidney was at the Potter household. Sidney and Rebecca sat on the patio, still wet from their dip in the pool. Mrs. Potter had just come outside to let them know dinner was almost ready. Both kids stood, and Rebecca handed Sidney a towel. "Here you go. We can probably go back into the pool after dinner, if my mom is okay with it."

"I am not okay with it," Mrs. Potter said, stepping out onto the patio. "It is a school night, young lady." Mrs. Potter turned to Sidney with a smile. "I placed some of Connor's old clothes in the bathroom. They might be too big, but I threw your clothes in the wash. You are more than welcome to jump in the shower before dinner."

Sidney smiled wide, almost skipping while heading towards the house. "Thank you! Thank you so much, Mrs. Potter!"

Sidney slipped past Mrs. Potter as she called out, "Please call me Linda when we are not at school!" She turned back towards her daughter who smiled ear to ear. "You children make me feel old some days."

With a giggle, Rebecca went skipping inside to change for dinner.

Sidney soaked up the warm shower and, even more so, the clean clothes. Stepping out of the bathroom, he could smell something absolutely delicious. Rebecca was helping her mom set the table when Sidney rounded the corner.

Linda turned to Sidney and said with a smile, "Have a seat. You can help yourself."

Sidney ended up having two plates full to the brim with food. The three of them made small conversation throughout the dinner, mostly talking about school and extracurricular activities. Once dinner had ended, Sidney insisted on helping clear the table. It wasn't until they were loading the dishwasher that things got really uncomfortable. Linda placed the last plate into the dishwasher before turning to Sidney. "Where is your mother?"

Sidney's eyes went wide. What was he supposed to say? The truth would get him in trouble with his mom, but a lie would not help him in this situation.

Linda sighed softly, "Stay the night, please. Connor is off at college, and we have the room. That way, I know you're safe."

Sidney nodded slowly. The idea of having somewhere clean and warm to sleep was intriguing, but his nerves were still there.

Linda placed a hand softly on his shoulder. "I know it is hard now, but talking about it is the best thing you can do. I can't completely help you if you don't talk about it. It will take time, but know I am here." She paused a moment, smiling down on him. "Becca!" she hollered out.

Rebecca popped her head around the corner.

"Sidney is going to stay the night because it is so late. Can you show him where Connor's room is? Then you, little lady, need to head to bed as well."

With a nod, both kids headed towards the other end of the house. Rebecca led Sidney to Connor's room. Before leaving the room, she turned with a smile and said, "Goodnight. I'm glad you're here." She closed the door softly behind her. Sidney walked around the room, uneasy, before deciding to try to settle down. He climbed into bed, but sleep was not coming easily. He watched the numbers on the bedside clock tick away until almost midnight. That was when he decided to try some fresh air. Tiptoeing throughout the house, Sidney made his way out to the back patio. The moon glowed brightly in the sky and reflected off the water of the pool, leaving Sidney in a trance-like state. He wasn't sure how long he stood there. He didn't even hear her approach, but by the time he realized she was there, it was too late.

Rebecca had gotten up to get a glass of water and noticed Sidney on the patio. She opened the door and called his name quietly. When she didn't get a response, she approached him from behind, continuously calling his name to gain his attention. Placing her hand on his shoulder, Sidney freaked out. He spun around quickly, scaring Rebecca at the same time. Rebecca stumbled to the side and lost her footing. Her head hit the corner of the wooden railing before falling into the pool. Sidney's heart raced as he looked over the pool. Frozen in place, eyes wide, he watched as the beaming light reflecting off the pool slowly faded into darkness. The water blended with the blood, giving a crimson effect. Sidney stood there in shock, the guttural scream of Linda being the only thing that could bring him back to reality.

CHAPTER SIX

"Let's start from the beginning, Sid. How did her death affect you?" Jack asked, crossing one leg over the other.

"I did not know what to do or what to say. The way her body just floated atop the pool; it was almost... peaceful," Sid responded, hands laying neatly in his lap, his expression blank. "It was seemingly her punishment."

"Punishment?"

"For helping me."

"You believe she deserved to be punished for helping you?"

"Why did I deserve to be helped?"

"Well, you were only eight at the time, Sid."

"And I was alone in the world, long before she came around."

"She's dead," is all the male officer said to the female officer who was watching over Sydney. His attempt to whisper to her was lackluster at best. As their eyes stared him down, pity crossed them. Pity was an emotion that Sidney did not like at all. He obviously knew that Rebecca was dead. He had watched it happen in slow motion, the blood cascading across the pool. There was no reason for them to whisper unless they were discussing a more sensitive matter. It was at that moment, he realized who exactly they were talking about.

Upon the accident, police attempted to track down Elvira Miller, Sidney's mother. Sidney couldn't tell them where she was because he had no idea. He told them of the last time he had seen her, standing in the doorway to their apartment. She had turned him away, which was very common. He discussed a few of the spots around town that he occasionally saw her going in or coming out of. He also knew a few names of people that she may be with. Unfortunately, Sidney only knew the first names because that was information he had obtained while eavesdropping. No information was ever shared with him willingly by his mother. The entire conversation with the officer was awkward for Sidney. He didn't want to talk to the officer out of fear from retaliation from his mother, but he felt like he had no choice, given what had happened to Becca.

He had overheard the officer asking if there were any open CPS cases against Sidney's mother, or if there had been any complaints. She wanted to know how that form of neglect could have gone on underneath anyone's nose. If anyone actually paid attention, they would see it was more common than they could ever believe. Social workers were understaffed and overworked. They never could get through their caseloads, and so many kids slipped through the cracks. Sidney had been one of those unfortunate kids.

It wasn't as if there hadn't been reports before. Plenty of teachers had reported in the short time he was in school. Elvira would get her "act" together long enough for the social worker to get out the door. There would be food in the fridge, clean clothes, and her feign attempt at love. Teachers stopped reporting out of fear when one of them was attacked by Elvira's drug dealer. Whenever she had to get it together, her use went down, and that made him deranged. He was losing money every day she had to play "mom," so he put an end to it as quickly as he could. He had to save his best customer.

The police had found Elvira, though, very easily. Her body had been rotting in the apartment since sometime after Sidney had left on Friday. Whispers throughout the precinct said it looked like an overdose. There was still a needle in her arm when they found her. There were only two things that his mother loved in this world, men and drugs. At least she died doing what she loved... and then it hit him. He could never go home. There wasn't a home to go to anymore. What was going to happen to him now? Where would he go? Death, it was all around him, shrouding him in a bleak, inescapable darkness. The grim reaper befriended him that day.

⇥ ⇥⇥ ⇥ ⇥⇥ ⇥

"How did your mother's death affect you?" Jack asked, making a notation in his notebook.

"It didn't, really. It wasn't like she was around much, anyways."

"Your mother and you never talked?"

"She would yell, and I would listen. I knew my place when it came to her. After my father..." Sid trailed off in thought.

"What about your father?"

"I sometimes wonder what he looked like, if I am like him in any way."

Jack scribbled in his notebook while nodding his head.

"His murder hit my mom really hard. Not catching his killer made it even worse. A hit and run... what a way to go, being left in the street like that. Elvira used to tell me to get out of her face, that she hated my face. I guess I looked like him, but when I looked at pictures, I didn't see it. She was eight months pregnant when he died, never done a drug in her life. I am told she was a good woman at one point in time, and he was a good man. I tried to be

47

good like him, you know?"

"In what ways do you believe you were 'good?'"

"Punishing those who deserved it, getting justice where others had failed. The system repeatedly failed me. I was only trying to help them." Sid leaned back, looking at the ceiling, recalling that day.

⪼ ⪼ ⪼ ⪼ ⪼

"Sidney, this is Margaret Bennett," the officer said, leading him to a gray-haired woman in sweats. Her eyes were the same color as her hair and appeared tired, but not from lack of sleep. Her age showed in her eyes.

"Hello, sweetheart." She smiled down at him. "Does he know?" she whispered to the officer.

The officer nodded slowly.

"You are going to come stay with me for a bit, okay? We can get you something to eat, if you want, before we head home."

Sidney just stared at her, puzzled. "Mrs. Potter said she would take care of me. She told me last night. Does she know where I am?"

Ms. Bennett leaned down to be eye level with him. He could see her eyes were full of pain... or was it pity? He didn't need the pity. "Mrs. Potter, unfortunately, can't take care of you right now, but I promise you will be safe with me."

Sidney glanced between the officer and the old woman and just nodded. If she was willing to give it a shot, what was wrong with him giving it a chance? He knew not to trust or get attached. People had a way of abandoning him.

Ms. Bennett placed a hand lightly on his back and led him out of the precinct and into a car. While helping him in, she said, "Would you like anything to eat?"

He just shook his head, feeling numb about the whole situation. His stomach was honestly still full from dinnertime. Plus, he wasn't quite sure what the catch would be with her. It would take time for Sidney to trust her.

It wasn't long before they arrived at a rather small house, just on the edge of the city. Ms. Bennett showed him around the house, ending at the room that would be his for the time being. She went over the house rules and encouraged him to talk about what happened, as that would help him heal. Heal... that was funny.

He spun in a circle, taking in his temporary room before turning to face her. "She went to Hell, you know," Sidney said plainly.

Ms. Bennett looked at him, shocked. She either wasn't expecting him to speak or was shocked that he opened up so fast. "Who?" she said, fumbling with her fingers, as if she was nervous of what his reply would be.

"My mom. That is where people always said she was going," he said as he crawled up into bed. It had been a long night, and he needed to get some rest.

Ms. Bennett was truly speechless by his words.

He laid down on his side, facing away from her. "It's okay, though. That is where bad people go."

"I'm sorry, honey," was the only thing she probably could think to say. She stepped out of the room and closed the door behind her.

He stared out of the window as daybreak peered over the horizon. Eventually, he let the darkness overcome him, and he slipped into a deep sleep.

⊁⊁ ⊁⊁ ⊁⊁ ⊁⊁ ⊁⊁

"We are a lot alike," Sid said, the corner of his mouth lifting into a smile.

"How were the two of you alike?"

"The way we looked at the world, and the way the world looked at us."

"How did you think the world looked at you?"

"Like I was a cockroach that needed to be exterminated, like a waste of space, a waste of oxygen... at least Elvira liked to say that a lot. She also said I was a bastard." Sid scoffed. "It was not my fault she was an unwed mother."

Jack just sat there silently, making notations in his notebook.

"Her favorite thing to say was that I would be the death of her."

"You know you did not cause her death, right?" Jack's head cocked to the side, quizzically.

"Physically, I did not. It was only a matter of time, though." His smile slowly turned into a smirk, his pale blue eyes boring into Jack. "There is a special spot in Hell for people like her. I have come to realize this in my short time on this planet. She would've honestly done almost anything to be rid of me. She just never had the guts to do anything, other than screw and shoot her life away until she couldn't handle her dose one night." He gave a chuckle to the idea of her being dead. "She can never escape me, though."

"Why do you say that?"

"I have a reserved spot next to her now. How much judgment do you think I am going to face for being the judge, jury, and executioner for so many people? I know I am not a good man, and I have proven it. It will be the greatest surprise ever for my dear mother, and to think of what it took for me to get back to her..."

>+>+>+>+>+

Over the next several years, Sidney bounced between homes, counselors, and therapists. He was never in one spot for too long, always faced with one excuse or another, explaining why he couldn't stay. There were always fake smiles and fictitious and devious actions. Unsurprisingly, most were in it for the money that it brought in. Foster kids paid big. Ms. Bennett ended up being the only kind soul to help one rooted in evil. Different medications, different therapies. Whenever Sidney spoke about the accident, his mother's death, or the life he had with her, he would speak about death as if it were his friend. Death intrigued him, and it became an unhealthy obsession.

He learned over time not to trust anyone. He would let others be the ones to open up to him, so he could see their true colors. The eyes truly did show straight into a person's soul, and Sidney got very good at reading people. For those who seemed to care, he would pull back the curtain just enough to let them peek in, but never enough where he would ever get hurt again. Eventually, Sidney ended up in the care of Arthur and Lucia Collins in Glenwood. In the past, the Collins family had taken in troubled youth. It was their "expertise," or so they thought. They felt they could get any child on the right path. They had a record of succeeding, but they had never had anyone like him. They were truly going to have their hands full with Sidney, and their lives would never be the same.

⇥ ⇥ ⇥ ⇥ ⇥

Over the next several years, Sidney bounced between homes, counselors, and therapists. He was never in one spot for too long, always faced with one excuse or another, explaining why he couldn't stay. There were always fake smiles and fictitious and devious actions. Unsurprisingly, most were in it for the money that it brought in. Foster kids paid big. Ms. Bennett ended up being the only kind soul to help one rooted in evil. Different medications, different therapies. Whenever Sidney spoke about the accident, his mother's death, or the life he had with her, he would speak about death as if it were his friend. Death intrigued him, and it became an unhealthy obsession.

He learned over time not to trust anyone. He would let others be the ones to open up to him, so he could see their true colors. The eyes truly did show straight into a person's soul, and Sidney got very good at reading people. For those who seemed to care, he would pull back the curtain just enough to let them peek in, but never enough where he would ever get hurt again. Eventually, Sidney ended up in the care of Arthur and Lucia Collins in Glenwood. In the past, the Collins family had taken in troubled youth. It was their "expertise," or so they thought. They felt they could get any child on the right path. They had a record of succeeding, but they had never had anyone like him. They were truly going to have their hands full with Sidney, and their lives would never be the same.

CHAPTER
SEVEN

Sidney sat on the steps of Edgeway Middle School, quietly waiting for his ride. Out of nowhere, Andy and Charlie appeared. Charlie plopped himself down beside Sidney before leaning back and lacing his fingers behind his head. "So, what do you think about the Mrs. Moore situation, Sid?" Charlie and Andy were the only ones who called him that. It honestly annoyed the shit out of him. That wasn't his name. Sidney always preferred to be called by his name and not Sid because it had been a family name, and it was the only piece he had left of the life he had before his mother died. He allowed only Andy and Charlie to call him Sid because they accepted him from the moment he stepped foot in the school. While others had shunned him or called him names, they embraced him like a brother. It was hard enough always being the new kid at different schools, but they made it a lot easier to settle in here.

Andy dropped himself on the other side of Sidney. "I think that old bat is going to get what she deserves." Andy gave him a slight nudge, as to make sure they had his attention. Sidney had a bad habit of spacing out and not realizing what was happening around him.

Sidney glanced between the two of them as the conversation bounced back and forth about what happened during English. The teacher, Mrs. Moore, had gotten too comfortable in her position at the school and was beginning to call some of the students bad names. Every little thing was stupid or uncalled for. Simple errors were egregious. When someone needed to use the restroom, she would make the student stand in the corner until the end of class for "attempting to disrupt the learning environment." When the bell rang, she would then make that student wait for everyone else to exit the classroom before allowing them to leave. Going to the bathroom in between classes was almost impossible, unless you wanted to be late, as there were only three minutes between each bell. Mrs. Moore was famous for falling asleep during class instead of teaching. She would make her students silently read while she "rested her eyes." But God forbid if a student fell asleep! Her actions became almost scary the farther into the semester they went.

Students had been secretly recording incidents since the beginning of the school year so that when there was enough evidence, they could take it to the superintendent. Today was that day, and each member of the class was asked to stay after so they could be interviewed by the principle, superintendent, and a few members of the school board. The last person on their list to talk to was Mrs. Moore herself.

At that moment, Lucia Collins pulled up in a gray SUV. With a honk, Sidney stood and headed for the vehicle. Charlie called after him, "See you tomorrow, dude!"

"Thanks for the convo!" Andy added, sarcastically, as always.

Sidney just waved them off before closing the door. They knew how he was; Sidney wasn't a big talker. He was more of the silent observer in the friendship. The boys did most of the talking, and they were okay with it. Lucia cleared her throat, snapping Sidney back to reality. "So, what happened today?"

Sidney shrugged in the passenger seat. "Just stuff with school."

"Did you get in trouble? It is okay if you did. I won't be mad. I know you boys can-"

He cut her off. "Mrs. Moore was turned in for her actions."

"Is that the English teacher with the attitude?"

"That's the one," he said with a nod.

"Well, I hope the situation resolves itself." Lucia smiled wide and began to bounce in her seat as she continued speaking, "Guess what is for dinner?"

"Chicken?"

"No, silly. Dinner was your pick tonight."

Sidney perked up in his seat and turned towards Lucia. "Did you make homemade meatballs?"

"And homemade spaghetti!" she said whimsically.

Lucia was an amazing cook. Barely anything in the house was processed. Everything was made from scratch and was as healthy as possible. Just the fact that he came home to a home cooked meal almost every night was magnificent. At previous homes, he would eat a lot of processed stuff, or they would leave you to fend for yourself. Growing up alone, he became very good at making the cup noodles. Living with Lucia had been the greatest thing to happen to him.

As they pulled into the driveway, the one downfall of living with her reared his ugly head. Arthur Collins yanked open Sidney's door, grabbed him by the arm, and tugged him out of the car. "What did you do now?"

Lucia came rushing out of the car, reaching out for Sidney. "No, no, no! He didn't do anything! He was helping his classmates."

Arthur's attention turned to Lucia. "You think he could have told us that last night? You know? Making plans ahead of time?" His head whipped back around to Sidney. "You know better than that, to be going off and doing your own thing! There are rules for a..."

"Arthur!" Lucia cut him off in his rant.

"What?" he snapped at her.

"Can we talk?" she said, gesturing towards Sidney. "Alone, please, and not out where our neighbors can hear."

Sidney jerked his arm away before grabbing his bag and heading towards the house. He could hear Lucia following close behind with Arthur on her tail. Sidney went straight for his room, and he could hear Lucia and Arthur beginning to discuss what had happened at school before he gently closed his door behind him. It wasn't as if he hadn't told Arthur about the issues with Mrs. Moore. It's just that he didn't care about what Sidney had to say. He often wondered why Arthur took in foster kids to begin with, or maybe he was just a bastard to only him? Sidney sat down at his desk and got to work on his homework. The last thing he wanted was a fight. Arthur was famous for picking fights, especially if he was irritated, like he seemed today. Some time had passed before a knock came to Sidney's door. "Come in," he said.

"Hey," a sweet voice came from the door as Lucia opened it. "Sorry about earlier. Arthur can sometimes be..."

"An asshole?" Sidney said plainly.

Lucia just gave him THE look. Sidney shrugged it off and turned back to his desk. "Well, dinner will be done in just a few, if you want to come set the table."

"Why do you put up with it?"

Sidney's back still faced Lucia, so he did not see the pain that crossed her face as she thought about his question. Instead of answering, she said, "Why don't I make some sweet tea for dinner? Go ahead and finish up what you are doing and come help." She turned swiftly and headed out of the room, leaving the door open behind her.

With a sigh, Sidney went to help prepare the table. Arthur was already on edge, and the last thing he wanted was to cause an even bigger mess.

With everyone seated at the table, small talk ensued, the "hello, how was your day" crap that happened every night. Sidney was always polite for the sake of Lucia. By the end of dinner, no one really had much to say. Arthur asked about the Mrs. Moore situation, and Sidney offered very little. Lucia, seeing that the conversation was dried up, perked up as she lifted herself from her seat. "How does pie sound? I made cherry."

Both of the men agreed that pie sounded amazing, so Lucia excused herself as she went to plate the slices. Sidney stood on cue, without a word, and began to clear the table as he did every night. But tonight would play out differently than what he had hoped. He gathered some of the dishes in his hands and, as he turned to head to the kitchen, Lucia appeared out of nowhere. Dishes collided, sliding away from both of them, the momentum of their movements making it impossible to stop what was transpiring before them. The crash of the dishes, the splat of the slices, and the red in Arthur's eyes all happened at what seemed like a snail's pace as Sidney looked on in horror.

In a flash, Lucia was shoved to the floor, and Sidney was up against the wall, held by his neck. He heard only the ringing in his ears as he watched the veins in Arthur's neck pulse, spittle flying from his mouth as he screamed at Sidney. He watched as Lucia scrambled from the floor and attempted to separate Arthur's hands from Sidney's neck. That only angered Arthur more, and he swung his arm around, hitting Lucia straight in the face. Lucia stumbled backwards, barely missing the edge of the table as she fell onto her butt. Sidney could handle Arthur smacking him around, but hitting Lucia, the one woman who cared, his angel, he was irate. With a swift motion, Sidney punched Arthur dead in the throat, feeling his hands release from his neck. Sidney bent down and propelled his shoulder into Arthur's abdomen, lifting like he had seen in football games, before dropping him on his back on the table. The two began to wrestle for control, and the only sound that finally came through was the sobs of Lucia as she sat helplessly looking on. The sobbing broke Sidney's heart, making him shove away from Arthur. He attempted to distance himself from the deplorable man.

What was going to happen from here? Sidney had never fought back before, but Arthur had never hurt Lucia, either. Flustered, Sidney whirled around and headed for the door as fast as he could. Air, he just needed air. Arthur still leaned against the table, a dumbfounded look plastered on his face from the whole situation. Lucia slowly rose from the floor, calling after Sidney. He slammed the door behind him as his brisk walk turned into a sprint. The farther away he got, the more her agonizing voice faded, and he felt he could almost take a breath. Sidney just kept running until he noticed a familiar spot, an old park that was in disarray. He slid down against a tree, facing away from the road in case someone came looking for him. He did not want to know what would happen when Arthur got his hands on him. He was finally able to take some slow, deep breaths. His eyes closed as he went over the events that had transpired earlier. He had no idea how long he sat there, but he realized that his phone in his pocket was vibrating. Glancing at the screen, he took in the seventeen missed calls from Lucia, none from Arthur. Was he out looking for him? Sidney knew he fucked up bad tonight, but there was no changing anything now. He would have to deal with the fallout of his actions, whether he wanted to or not. That was when his phone started to vibrate again, Lucia's name flashing across the screen. He needed to deal with this now. He needed to know how bad it was so he could weigh his options. He would either need to run and never come back or return home and face the consequences. He swiped and placed the phone against his ear.

"Sidney?" Lucia choked back a sob. "Please tell me you are safe."

He sat in silence for a moment, listening for any movement around him before responding, "Yes, I am."

"Just come home. It will all be okay," her voice strained.

"No, it won't... You know it won't," Sidney stammered. "Where is he now?"

The sigh was faint, "He just went to bed. He didn't say a word." Silence passed between them as they sat on the phone together. Minutes passed before Lucia pleaded with him again. "Please... just come home."

If his heart wasn't shattered before, it was now. Lucia was his only weakness in this life. He would do anything to make her happy, to keep her... safe. That was more obvious now than it had ever been. He would do absolutely anything for her. "I will be home in a few."

"Thank you," she said with an almost inaudible sigh of relief.

He could hear her smile through her words, and it delighted him. No matter what had happened, having Lucia happy made him happy. Hanging up, he placed his phone back in his pocket and began his walk home. He hadn't realized how far he had actually run until 15 minutes had passed and his phone was vibrating once more. Without looking, he swiped and put it up to his ear.

"Almost there, coming up the st..."

"I'm coming to get you. I'm hopping in the car now." Lucia's voice was taut.

"What's going on?"

"Where are you?" Lucia said, almost cutting him off.

"What. Is. Going. On?" He wasn't going to give up that easily. Her voice gave no hints to what might have transpired at home.

"We are going to Bella's house for the night. We just have to let Arthur calm down, give him a little bit of space." There was silence over the phone as headlights appeared before Sidney. "I see you," and then nothing as Lucia hung up the phone.

The car slowly rolled to a stop next to Sidney, and he hopped in beside Lucia. She stared straight ahead as she accelerated and headed out of the neighborhood. Sidney studied her face as they rolled under the streetlights. No sound or movement came from inside the car. It wasn't until Lucia had to make a left turn that he saw the bruise that was forming under her left eye. Before jumping to conclusions, he needed to run over tonight's events once more. Lucia had gotten hit in the clash between Sidney and Arthur, but he remembered, clear as day, that she was hit on the right side of her face.

"Hey!" Lucia screeched as Sidney flipped on the overhead light of the car, the mark on her right cheek showing brightly.

"Did he hit you?" Anger boiled deep inside him, and he was trying not to explode.

"It... it was an ac-accident." She shook her head as tears formed in her eyes.

He flipped off the overhead light because if he looked at the mark on her any longer, he was going to hop out of this car to hunt him down and kill him. "What happened?" He crossed his arms over his chest as he sat there, attempting to slow his rising heart rate.

With a sigh, Lucia finally gave him some answers. "He came storming out of our room about ten minutes after I talked to you." She choked back a sob. "I attempted to talk with him. He... he was just so angry. I..."

"No more, please," Sidney said, laying his hands on his legs as he lowered his head. He took a deep breath, trying so hard to keep his emotions in check. Hurting her, making her relive something like that, he wasn't going to do that to her. No, he was going to make it all better. They sat in silence the rest of the way to Lucia's sister's house. Bella was married to a cop, and Arthur never pulled anything in front of them. They would be safe there for the night, and it would give Sidney time to make a plan. Arthur had to go.

CHAPTER EIGHT

Bella didn't ask any questions when she opened the door to Lucia and Sidney. It was just after eleven when they arrived. Lucia must have called her before picking him up because she was expecting them, dressed in her pajamas, with tea in hand. Thankfully, Carlos was already asleep for the night, so Lucia wasn't going to get the third degree from him like she had in the past. Sidney was offered tea as well, but he opted for a pillow instead. Today was just absolutely draining, and he needed some rest. Bella showed Sidney to the spare room before disappearing back downstairs to Lucia. He stripped down to his boxers to try to get as comfortable as possible before throwing back the covers and hopping onto the memory foam mattress. As he laid in the bed, staring at the ceiling, he listened to the whispering happening between the sisters.

"You can't go back to him, Lucy. Not again."

"Where would I go? I don't have a job, and I have to take care of Sidney somehow."

A huff came from Bella. "You could come here. We have the room, you know."

A loud sigh came from Lucia. "No, we couldn't. I can't uproot him any more than he already has in his life. He has his friends. He finally has a life with us. You know what he has been through. You and Carlos are the only ones that should understand what uprooting him would do. I've confided in you two and asked for advice with him. This is one thing where I don't need your advice. I won't be putting him through something like that again."

"What he's been through?! Jesus Christ!" A harsh whisper came from Bella. "What about what he is going through now? What kind of life is it to be living this way? Don't *you* think he deserves better? Don't you deserve better?"

"Arthur probably won't even remember it, by tomorrow morning." Lucia always dodged the hard questions when it came to Arthur. Changing the subject and deflecting had become second nature to her.

Anyone listening in could hear the irritation in Bella's voice as it raised, "So, excuses? What would mami say if she were still alive?"

"Isabella!" Lucia shouted at her.

"Lucia!" Bella countered in a snarky tone.

At that moment, a door closed near Sidney, and footsteps started to descend down the stairs. Sidney sat up from his bed and tiptoed to the door to try to hear better.

"Lucia?" A groveled, sleepy voice said. "What in the hell...?"

"Tell him," said Bella.

"It was an accident."

"Like hell it was, Lucy!" Bella was yelling at this point.

"Shh! You'll wake up Sidney!"

Sidney just shook his head, eyes rolling. Lucia should know better. He had been caught so many times eavesdropping in on conversations, especially ones that she did not want him to know about. He had done it so many times that he got good at sneaking around.

"Did he hurt Sidney as well?" came the voice again. Sidney figured it was Carlos, as he would be the only other person in the house at this time.

"Sidney didn't say he was hurt... it just, ugh... it all happened so fast. Should I check on him? Oh God, what if he is hurt?"

"Did Sidney say anything to you, Bella?" Carlos asked.

"No, but I did give a quick once over and didn't see anything," Bella replied.

"Tonight was different," Lucia said with a sigh. "I've never seen Sidney so upset. He fought back against Arthur."

"Good on him for protecting you and himself, but by the looks of you," Carlos sighed, "You are not going back. I won't let you. Not this time."

"But..." Lucia said, defeated. It was now two against one.

"We can get everything settled in the morning. Right now, everyone needs to try to get some rest. Sidney upstairs?" Someone must have nodded because Sidney didn't hear a response. Carlos ended with, "Good, let him get some rest, and you as well, Lucia. We can talk about it tomorrow so I can help you the best I can."

With that, footsteps started up the stairs, and Sidney rushed back to his bed so he could pretend to be asleep. It was a good thing he did because the door opened and a voice came from the darkness. "Sidney?" Lucia waited a moment before closing the door and heading to another room down the hall. Sidney laid there for a few minutes thinking over tonight's events once more. He was going to put an end to this once and for all, with or without Lucia's help. Sidney gave in after a while and let his body relax before letting the darkness swallow him into a much-needed deep sleep.

The morning started early and passed by quickly. Sidney went with the motions of everything, telling his side of the story to Carlos and then a uniformed officer. Lucia refused to press charges, which he knew would be the case. She never pressed charges against him and never would. She just kept saying that she wanted to go home. Even when Carlos and Bella tried talking her out of it, she would just shake her head and repeat that she needed to be home. Sidney just sat silently when he wasn't answering questions, planning where he would go from here. Arthur needed to go, but the how was going to be the most difficult part. Without being close to him for at least a short period of time, they might not ever be rid of him permanently. When asked what he wanted to do, he said he wanted to go back to the house. Lucia was shocked at his response, as he always voiced his disdain for Arthur. Little did she know that Sidney needed Arthur as close as possible to make the plan he was concocting work. So, it was finalized, even with Carlos and Bella disagreeing with them leaving. Sidney and Lucia packed up to head home.

Upon returning home, Arthur was distraught. Crying, he begged for forgiveness from Lucia, who would simply accept his words as fact without any question. It was the same as always, flowers and tears, making dinner, and then a back rub. They would cuddle on the couch and fall asleep draped around one another. The apology to Sidney was less sincere and more of an act than anything. He said he was sorry with a pat on the back, calling Sidney his buddy. Arthur reminded Sidney that he never meant to hurt him, but that he needed to learn his place in this house and show more respect to him. Sidney had to bite his tongue and just nod with a smile. Anything more could cause another explosion, and he needed to be here to make any sort of plan work. Within a few hours, the house was running as if nothing had happened the night before. Sidney stayed in his room and kept to himself. Dinner was quiet, with very little conversation passed around the table, and night came very quickly. Hours turned to days, and days turned to weeks that Arthur played the good, dutiful husband and father. Lucia seemed none the wiser, and Sidney just stayed out of the way, biding his time, methodically planning. Then came the day that Sidney would remove Arthur from the picture once and for all.

Lucia was to be gone for the day - Bella had invited her out for a girl's day. Bella and Lucia tried to get together at least once a month to do something. Sometimes it was at the house or at Bella's, but most of the time, it was in the city so the girls were gone the entire day. Lucia had to be away for this to work, and Sidney made sure that Lucia was aware that he was going to go hang with Andy and Charlie. They had breakfast together as a family, like they did every Sunday, and Lucia headed on her way while Arthur headed outside to do yard work. Lucia had left food in the microwave for Arthur to have lunch, like she always did. Sidney acted as if he was leaving and waited for the house to be empty before slipping quietly back inside. He would have just over 2 hours before Arthur would sit down for lunch, which meant he needed to complete his tasks swiftly and without error.

Sidney started with the food. Arthur was highly allergic to shellfish. Just the smallest contact caused him to puff up. Whenever they ate seafood, it was on a night that Arthur had to work late, and Lucia would have extra time to clean up afterwards. Sidney took a single frozen shrimp out of the freezer and proceeded to rub it all over the plate of food that had been saved for Arthur before placing it back into the freezer bag. That would be enough to cause a mild reaction. Heading into the master bathroom, Sidney grabbed the bottle of antihistamines and poured about half the bottle into his hand before replacing the bottle. A door closed, setting Sidney on edge. He listened for footsteps, and as they headed up the stairs, he escaped into his room. He only hoped that Arthur would make his way back outside quickly. What he didn't expect was for Lucia to open his door and find him there.

"Sidney!" She huffed, placing a hand on her chest. "You startled me. What are you doing home?"

Slowly, Sidney slipped his hand into his pocket, letting the pills fall before pulling out his phone. "Forgot my phone," he said, waving it between the two of them. "I figured I should have it on me in case someone needed to get in touch with me."

Lucia smiled, "Well, thank you for coming back for it."

"And what are you doing?" Sidney said quizzically.

"Your sneakers have holes in them, and you never answer me when I ask what size you wear. Figured I'd find out myself and get you a new pair."

"Eleven and a half, and I don't like…"

"High tops, I know," Lucia said, cutting him off. Gesturing towards the hallway she said, "You want a ride?"

"That's okay. Charlie and Andy are on their way here, and we are going to walk together."

"Okay, have fun!" Smiling, Lucia turned and headed out of the house.

Sidney waited for complete silence before heading onto his next task. Heading back into the kitchen, he took the pills from his pocket and ground them into a powder. Once the pills were fine with no chunks, Sidney poured a glass of sweet tea and mixed the powder into the tea. He continued until there were no specs left and placed the glass into the fridge. For a measure of safety, Sidney creeped to a window in the study to put eyes on Arthur. Sure enough, Arthur was on the riding lawn mower with his headphones on. He had less than half of the yard done, so Sidney had more than enough time, as long as nothing went wrong. With the first part of his plan done, he would move onto the hard part. If this messed up, there would be no recovering from it. He would have to scrap the whole plan and try another day. First step was the circuit breaker, he needed to turn off the power to the master bedroom. Once he had the power off, he grabbed the tools he needed and headed upstairs. Stripping the outlet was the easy part. He had just looked up what to look for when fixing an outlet and planned to do the opposite. He even went as far as offering to help Arthur with little home improvement tasks so he could learn more. Arthur soaked up any free labor he could get. Poor bastard didn't even know he was showing Sidney just how to be his undoing. He stripped the wires inside the outlet and made them stick out in a way that wasn't obvious. The next step was to place the curtain in front of the outlet. This would not only hide that area on the wall that Sidney tampered with, but would also be the perfect conductor for the fire. Arthur would turn on the fan, causing electricity to flow. It was the perfect plan. He made sure to have a backup by stripping the wire to the fan close to the plug, just in case the outlet failed. With everything in place, Sidney cleaned up what he could and put everything back where it was. Now, Sidney would need to wait. For a measure of good faith, Sidney headed to the study at the rear of the house to peak out of the window. Laying eyes on Arthur, he was able to tell that he was just about done with the lawn. He had maybe ten minutes before Arthur would come inside. He headed down to the basement at that moment and would let the events play out.

Right on time, Arthur came into the house for lunch, heated his food, and grabbed the glass of sweet tea that was already poured and ready. Sidney sat on the steps in the basement, listening closely. First came the coughing, next, the glass slamming on the table. Sidney prayed Arthur would finish off his drink. If he didn't, there would be a chance that this would not work. Footsteps ascended up the staircase. He knew at this point in time, Arthur would realize he was having an allergic reaction and attempt to stop it. He would grab his Epi-pen from the bathroom and proceed to take more antihistamine, not knowing his tea held twenty times the normal dose already. The Epi-pen would increase his heart rate, and in turn, begin to make Arthur tired. Mixing that with an abnormal level of antihistamines, Arthur was going to be taking a nice nap and, hopefully, have some nasty side effects. Sidney headed up the steps slowly and silently to lay eyes on the table and, sure enough, the glass of tea was empty.

"What did you make me for lunch?" Arthur yelled into the phone, his words forced, followed by silence for a moment. "Well, I'm going to lie down. Maybe I came in contact with something outside... mhm... yep... alright, enjoy your time with Bella. I will call if I need you."

Jackpot! Stealthily, Sidney made his way back down into the basement. Arthur would head into his room next and flip on his fan before laying down. Neither one of them slept without a fan. Sidney flipped the breaker to allow power back to the master bedroom before slipping out the back door. Now he just prayed he did enough planning and research for everything to pay off. Sidney began to run as fast as he could. He needed to be at the park when all this went down. Charlie and Andy would be his alibi, if he needed one. If everything went according to his plan, he wouldn't, and this would be labeled as an accident.

Arriving at the park, Sidney placed eyes on Charlie and Andy. He approached them, relaxed, and the three of them began to shoot the shit like they always did. Andy and Charlie had always been obsessed with football. Sidney wasn't a big sports person, but he enjoyed playing ball with his friends. Time passed slowly, at least it felt that way to him. The three boys juggled between throwing the ball, wrestling, and snacking on the food that Andy's mom always sent for them. Two and a half hours later, his phone rang. Stepping away from the guys, he slid the phone to answer. Before even placing it to his ear, he could hear Lucia sobbing on the other end. His heart began to race, his palms becoming sweaty. This was the only hard part about the plan, hurting Lucia if he had succeeded, but Sidney would help make it better.

"Where are you?" She forced out the words before sobbing once more. Sirens could be heard in the background.

"I'm at the park with the guys still." Andy threw the ball at Sidney's feet as Sidney waved him off. Andy came jogging over and grabbed the ball, nudging Sidney, but he waved him off once more. Andy threw the ball at Charlie and gave Sidney space. "What's going on? Are you okay?" He could easily make himself sound concerned for Lucia. Being concerned for her was never an act, it was pure and real.

"Arthur... there was a f-" Lucia began to

sob once more. Loud noises, shouting and hissing from what sounded like machinery, broke through and almost covered her sobs.

Sidney listened as a ruffling sound came across the phone before Isabella's voice came through. "Carlos is on his way to grab you. Please send him a message where exactly you are so he isn't searching for you. There was a fire at your house." A heavy sigh came from her. "Arthur was in the fucking house..."

"He didn't make it out?" Sidney forced himself to sound sincere.

Bella confirmed, "He didn't make it out."

With his back turned to Andy and Charlie, a sinister smiled crept across his face. His pale blue eyes gleamed in the descending sunlight as adrenaline coursed through his body, a victory before him for the taking.

CHAPTER NINE

"What made you kill him?" Jack said as he crossed one leg over the other.

"What made me do it? Nothing. I wanted him dead. It was as simple as that. He didn't deserve another day on this Earth, but it took me a while to plan it."

"Why did you make it look like an accident?"

"The main reason, I didn't want him to know what was coming. If someone were to come at you with a gun or a knife, you could fight back. Too many variables if he had the opportunity to fight back. I thought long and hard about how I wanted him to die. I took many precautions and thought of backups."

"Was the fish supposed to kill him?"

"No, not necessarily. If it did, great. If it

didn't, it was just one piece of the puzzle. I wanted him to wake up to the house on fire. I wanted him to feel pure terror, knowing there was no escaping. I wanted him to suffer the way I had suffered by his hands. The way..." Sid's face twisted.

"The way Lucia had suffered," Jack said, laying his hands in his lap, finishing for him.

"He deserved what he got and so much more for what he did to her."

"And what about after he died? How did everything seem to work out then?"

>+>+>+>+>+

It was almost a week before Lucia left her room at Bella's house. Carlos had been taking Sidney back and forth to school every day, even though it had been a forty-minute drive one way. Carlos said Sidney needed some normalcy to cope, and Sidney wanted to go to school. Carlos had insisted on driving him, instead of ripping Sidney out of his school for a new one in the midst of a tragedy. Being near Lucia was very hard at this point in time. Just knowing that he was the cause of her pain was almost too much to bear. He knew that time would help her, and her life would be better without Arthur's abuse.

It took less than two weeks for the fire marshal to return with his report. The fire had been electrical and thus ruled an accident. Arthur's official cause of death was smoke inhalation. He had been found in the hallway, which meant he had woken up when it was indeed too late to escape. Sidney left his expression blank when anyone discussed Arthur, even though internally, he was cheering.

Three weeks after Arthur's passing, a funeral was held. Sidney was hoping after the funeral, things would return to normal, at least as normal as it could get. In a sense, Lucia attempted to do just that. She never returned to the property. She began to look for a place for Sidney and herself, stating she felt like a burden on her sister. When asked what she wanted to do with items that survived the fire, she said she wanted them to be given away. Bella insisted she at least attempt to sell items so they would have money to get a new place. Whatever was salvageable from the house, Bella had sold for Lucia, which was mostly outdoor items. Bella and Carlos attempted to comb through what little remained of the house, not recovering much in the end. Lucia kept saying she didn't want anything from the house, that they would figure it out. Her words exactly, "No point in holding on to the past when there is no changing it." The community rallied together and raised money for Lucia and Sidney. With the money that was raised, and what little they got from the items that sold, Lucia was able to rebuild however she wanted. Bella helped find a small three-bedroom house a few blocks away from Sidney's school, as Lucia refused to make him change districts in the middle of the school year.

The new place was heavenly. The landlord refused to take the first couple months of rent, as he wanted to help in any way that he could. Lucia and Sidney settled nicely in the new place. With Arthur gone, Charlie and Andy felt more comfortable coming around and began to hang at Sidney's house whenever they could. Before, Charlie and Andy came over only once. Arthur had been drinking and lost his mind over the fact that Sidney had friends over. Charlie and Andy never returned after that, insisting they hang out at other places. Sidney didn't mind that. In fact, he loved the idea of not having to be home around Arthur. He told Charlie and Andy about everything but asked them not to repeat it. The three boys would share many secrets growing up together. Lucia eventually confided in Sidney that it made their new place feel like home when she saw him laughing and having fun with his friends. She never talked about Arthur, and Sidney didn't press the issue. It became an unspoken understanding.

With Arthur gone, Lucia had to find a job to help support the two of them. A local vet office hired her without any experience, which was, "A stroke of good luck for them," Lucia had said. Her happiness slowly returned with every passing day, and it seemed like it was perfect, being just the two of them.

>>> >>> >>> >>> >>>

"Did you ever think about telling the truth to Lucia?" Jack leaned towards Sid.

"At first, every day," Sid said as he picked at a nail.

"And then?"

"He got what he deserved, even if she didn't understand. She had been put through enough by him. Why cause her any more pain and burden her with what I did for us? We were better off without him." Sid's movement halted as he stared at his hand, a drop of blood appearing on his cuticle. His eyes shifted to Jack, who leaned back in his seat, scribbling into his notebook. "You think I was possessive over Lucia, which is the complete opposite of how I felt. But it is women like her who need to be protected from evil like Arthur."

"Like you protected Jenna?" Jack's eyebrows raised as his pen tapped once on the paper.

"Her, I was possessive about. I wasn't going to share her, and I would protect her from anything, just like I had Lucia." Sid stared dead into Jack's eyes.

"If you wanted to protect her, why did you confess to her? Why 'burden her,' as you say?"

"She needed to know the truth about evil, and I showed her true evil... and yet, she still stands beside me. She started to ask questions, so I gave her answers. She showed strength, and I trusted her."

Jack shook his head. "But she asked questions after Ralph's death."

Sid gave a huff, "I had just met her at that point in time. Would you tell a

81

stranger your dirty little secrets? If it wasn't for Ralph's death, I don't think we would have ever spoken."

꘏ ꘏ ꘏ ꘏ ꘏

"Dude, dude, dude, DUDE!" Andy screeched as he ran up to Charlie and Sidney.

"What?" Charlie responded, glancing out of the corner of his eye as Sidney turned towards Andy.

Andy took a moment to get air into his lungs before saying, "It's Abby, man! She's pregnant!"

"Oh, shit..." Sidney's eyes widened as he turned his attention to Charlie. Charlie and Abigail Kelman had gone out a handful of times to the local arcade to hang out recently. He really liked her, and he thought that there was something developing between the two of them. Sidney watched as Charlie's eyes scrunched in confusion.

"Why didn't you tell us things were getting good with Abby?" Andy said, waggling his eyebrows as he gave him a nudge on his shoulder.

Charlie's head shook slowly, and the other two realized that Charlie was lost.

"You didn't...?" Sidney said, eyebrows raising in reference to the dirty deed.

"God, no."

Andy got hyped up, "Shit, who's kid is it, then? Any idea?"

Charlie shook his head again. "No idea. Can you imagine having a kid at

82

fourteen?"

Sidney leaned up against his locker, arms dangling in front of him as he held onto his backpack. "Dodged a bullet with that one, then." Turning his attention to Andy, Sidney continued, "How did you find out?"

"She passed out in gym. Someone must have taken her to a doctor or something. I guess she sent a text to someone who told someone and blah, blah. You know how girls are..." Andy said as he waved his hand between them. "Between baby drama and the new girl, man, there is a lot happening in this school."

The boys continued the discussion of girls, including the new one as they headed out of the building. Sidney couldn't wrap his head around someone his age even being interested in sex, let alone risking having a kid this young. He hadn't yet seen the new girl because he had been late to school due to an appointment. There was always tomorrow. The three boys sat down on the steps as Charlie and Andy waited for rides home. Sidney walked now that he lived just a few blocks, and with Lucia working, he liked to just chill with his friends before they all had to go their separate ways for the night. Once Charlie and Andy left, Sidney stood to head home but stopped when he saw movement out of the corner of his eye. He dropped his bag down to not make it obvious as he looked back to be nosy. It was Abby sneaking from the side of the school into the building. His heart actually hurt for her. He couldn't even begin to imagine what she was going through. Swinging his bag up on his shoulder, he headed back towards the school with the intention of letting Abby know she still had a friend if she needed one. Slipping into the school, he caught Abby rounding the corner and headed in that direction. Before reaching the end of the hallway, he heard voices.

"What are you doing here?" came a male voice.

"I don't know what to do. My parents are so upset. I needed to see you, to talk to you," Abby's pleading voice responded to the man. Sidney figured the voice must be the father, but he didn't recognize it.

"You shouldn't have come here," came the voice again.

From the sound of Abby's voice, she had started to cry. "I didn't know where else to go. I can't take care of a baby on my own."

"Do you realize what would happen to me? I would lose my job! I refuse to go to prison over you, so get rid of it!"

"You told me you loved me! You told me you cared!" Abby began to sob, "Please don't go!" she screamed as footsteps headed towards Sidney. Sidney pressed himself flush against the wall as a figure stormed by. His eyes told him all he needed to know. Mr. Smithinson, the principal, was the father of Abby's baby.

>+> >+> >+> >+> >+>

"It seems you find yourself drawn to people in trouble. Why do you think that is?" Jack asked, as he leaned to the side in his chair.

"It is almost like a nagging voice in my head. If I can help, why not?" Sid shrugged.

"So, you believe that killing the people you have... helped?" Jack stared at Sid quizzically.

Sid's hand waved out in between them as he spoke, "In the eyes of most, it is wrong. It is a solution that is unconventional but quick and efficient."

"Why not try to go to the proper authorities, especially in the case of your principal?"

Sid's face twisted as he huffed at Jack. "You're kidding me, right? Show me where they actually help? The few who actually get help, tell me they are better off having a case dragged out and having to deal with the traumas over and over again. Or, even better, the scum gets a plea deal and a slap on the wrist." Sid rolled his eyes, slouching down into his chair.

"What about the families of those you killed?"

Sid slowly sat back, and his eyes wandered around the room as he thought about that question. He took a deep breath before responding, "I will get what I deserve in the end..."

CHAPTER TEN

Sidney kept his body pressed against the wall as he watched the principal exit the building from a side door. All that remained in the school seemed to be the quiet sobs coming from Abby. So badly, he wanted to comfort her, but what would he say, "Sorry you screwed the principal, and he turned out to be a douche bag?"

At that moment, a phone rang. "Hello," Abby spoke out. "I'm at the school. I needed to grab a book for... but..." A gasp escaped her lips. "Mom, Charlie's not... come pick me up, please."

Sidney hurried towards the locker room as footsteps headed towards him. He did not want to be seen. Whatever was happening, he needed to give Charlie a heads up or a warning. Sliding his phone from his pocket, he quickly selected "Charlie" from his phone. Charlie picked up on the second ring. "Charlie! Something is going on…"

"I can't talk right now. Abby's dad just showed up here. I'll call you later." Silence followed as Charlie hung up. He was concerned for his friend but had no idea how he could help him. The only thing he could think of was getting Mr. Smithinson to confess. He knew confronting him head on might be dangerous, depending on how far Mr. Smithinson was willing to go to keep this covered up. Not only was this shit-stain stupid enough to cheat on his wife, he did it with an underage student. His affair would ruin his life if it came out, but Abby didn't deserve this at all. One way or another, Ralph Smithinson would be an honest man.

Sidney made his way home, as fast as he could, all the while messaging Andy about the Charlie situation. Andy lived only a few blocks from Charlie, which would allow him to head over as backup, if needed. Sidney decided it was time to do a little digging into the principal, time to see what kind of man he truly was. Time seemed to pass slowly as he clicked away on his keyboard. Suddenly, his name was called by Lucia. Sidney glanced at the time in the corner of the computer screen, blinking a few times before realizing that four hours had passed since he had sat down. "What's up?" he yelled back at her.

"Dinner, silly!"

With a sigh, Sidney closed out of everything before heading down to the table. Rounding the corner to the dining room, Lucia stood right in front of him with a smile on her face. He bounced back, eyebrows raised. "Chipper much?"

"Well, tonight is a special occasion." She placed a hand on his back, leading him to his seat. Laying on the table was a buffet of junk food: pizza, wings, soda, fried dough, you name it.

"Okay...?" he said questionably as he took his seat. Plopping down across from him, her smile widened as they just stared at one another. "So? Spill."

Gesturing towards the food in front of them, she announced, "I got the job and the raise that came with it!"

Sidney smiled widely. "Congratulations! See? I knew you could do it."

A cell phone rang and interrupted their celebrations. Both pulled out their phones, but it was Sidney who stood, motioning towards his phone as he left the table to answer. Once he was in the other room, he answered, "What's up?"

"Dude, it's a shit storm over here!" Andy screamed into the phone. "Oh, shit!"

"What is going on?" Sidney tried to keep his voice low so Lucia didn't hear.

"Hud just sucker punched Mr. Kelman!" Andy seemed to be almost cheering as he watched what unfolded in front of him. Hudson Cooper, better known as Hud, was Charlie's father. If Hud and Mr. Kelman were fighting, he knew it had to do with the Abby situation.

"Can I get more than just that?" Sidney said, a bit louder, frustrated.

"So, Mr. Kelman showed up furious, I

guess. They were inside talking for some time. Then, Abby and Mrs. Kelman showed up, and there were accusations thrown around. Charlie tried to say he didn't mess with Abby like that, and Abby attempted to back him up. I got here when Hud was trying to get Mr. Kelman to leave. Mr. Kelman started to hurl insults and decided to call Charlie a 'motherless mouth-breather,' and that was that." Screaming could be heard in the background as Andy spoke. It was only a small pause before he spoke again. "And... the cops are here."

Through the phone, Sidney heard Hud's voice, "Go home, Andy!"

With a chuckle, Andy continued, "And now I'm leaving because I will never not do what Hud says, ever again."

Sidney looked up to the doorway as a shadow appeared. Lucia was glaring at him with a hand on her hip and the other holding her phone. "I got to go, keep me updated." Without waiting for a response, Sidney hung up and smiled at Lucia.

Lucia held up her phone between them, showing Wanda Marshall's name across the screen. "We both want to know what is going on." Lucia waved her phone in her hand. "And she wants to know where her son is."

Following Lucia back to the table, Sidney sat and explained as much as he could without disclosing the principal situation. Sidney stuck up for Charlie and swore that he had nothing to do with it. The entire time that they talked, including "the talk" about protection and such, Sidney was thinking of ways to help

Charlie and Abby. By the time he made it back to his room, he had figured out a way to communicate with Mr. Smithinson that would give him a chance to come clean. It would be quick and easy. Sidney typed out a brief but blunt note on his laptop. Printing it out, he stuffed it in an envelope and then into his backpack for safe keeping.

The next morning came quickly, and Sidney made his way to the school earlier than normal to place the note in Mr. Smithinson's mailbox at school without being seen. Unfortunately, Ms. Hayes was there early as well. He stood just outside the office, waiting for the perfect moment when Ms. Hayes turned her back to work on something. Silently, he slid in and out, undetected. The note gave Ralph Smithinson forty-eight hours to come forward about his involvement with his student or face consequences. Forty-eight hours passed, and Ralph stayed silent.

Abby returned to school and kept her head down around everyone. She didn't seem the same. Rumors floated around the school. Some stated that she was forced to get an abortion, others said she made the whole pregnancy up. No matter what was said, Sidney knew that Ralph had taken advantage of Abby, and he didn't deserve to stay at the school.

Over the next few weeks, Sidney stood silently around, watching and planning the perfect punishment for a monster like him. Nothing seemed good enough for a punishment. It wasn't until lunchtime, two weeks later, that Sidney was able to plan what would happen to Mr. Ralph Smithinson.

"Hey, Charlie!" Andy whispered in a hushed, sharp tone. His head jarred towards the other side of the cafeteria. In walked Abby, head hung low. Her face was more pale than normal, she didn't seem to shine like she used to.

Charlie sighed, placing his hands over his face.

"What? I thought the two of you were getting along," Andy said, shoving chips into his mouth.

"Just don't say anything, alright?" Charlie started, head continuing to hang. He rubbed his eyes like he had a headache before continuing. His volume became very hushed. "Her dad forced her to get an abortion. It was either that, or she could leave."

"As in, they were going to kick her out?" Sidney said, leaning into the table, trying to keep his voice low. He was shocked that they would even do something like that.

"They finally believed it wasn't my kid." As another classmate walked by, Charlie leaned in farther, voice going even softer, "They planned to take her out of town to that Healthy Living clinic." Running his fingers through his hair, he sighed once more. "I know there was a meeting here last week. Her parents were asking the school for help through this situation, and the abortion-to-be was brought up. Abby said she was so embarrassed by the way her parents handled it all. The meeting consisted of the guidance counselor, the principal, and one of Abby's teachers. She won't say who the dad is, though. All she told me was he was older, and that she wasn't going to get him in trouble for her mistakes."

Sidney sat back in his seat as his eyes wandered over to Abby. She was alone and broken. Anyone could see it, if they looked close enough. Ralph didn't deserve to live. He deserved to die, just like Abby had on the inside.

The next several days went by slowly. Sidney studied Ralph and his movements and came across a nice bit of information while hovering around the main office. Ralph was deathly allergic to wasps, and it just so happened that a nest was outside in the staff parking lot. The nest was hanging dangerously low on a very flimsy branch. He needed maintenance to take care of it as soon as possible or call someone to take care of it. Ralph stated he was worried about children getting stung. Sidney laughed at that comment, knowing full well how Ralph cared for his students. He would have to make his plan quickly, if he was going to use the nest to his advantage. This plan, he knew, was going to be very rushed and possibly would not work in his favor, but it was a risk he was willing to take.

His first step was to make sure the work request never reached maintenance. Thankfully, all work requests were filled out on paper and placed into the mailbox for the supervisor to pick up. All it took was one distracted Ms. Hayes, and Sidney slipped in and out of the office with the work request in hand. Next would be the hardest part of the plan, and the most likely part to fail. He would have to return to school later that night, when no one was around, to see what he could do to manipulate the hive. From the end of the school day until his return after nightfall, Sidney studied and read anything he could about wasps. He learned that provoking them could cause them to swarm and attack. The problem was getting them to swarm at the right moment.

Hours passed before he was finally able to return to the school to finalize his plan. Under the cover of darkness, he began to execute his quickly devised plan. The nest was low enough that it was roughly eye level with him. Messing with the branch meant there was a chance of the wasps attacking him, or worse off, leaving a trail for a police officer to follow. Sidney wandered around the parking area as he ran facts through his head. The nest just needed to be disturbed with Ralph near it. Getting Ralph near the spot would be rather difficult, seeing as he already knew the wasps were there. His eyes continued to scan his surroundings as he walked to think. The next moment, he had it all figured out. Tomorrow, Ralph would die.

The night passed quickly, and a new dawn appeared over the horizon. Sidney left his house that day, confident that justice would be served, swift and harsh. Throughout the night, he thought about how to lure Ralph close enough to the wasps. Sidney figured if Ralph truly thought someone was going to spill the beans about his illicit "love affair" with an underage student, he would do anything to keep it a secret. So, he devised a letter that said:

Ralph Smithinson,

Meet me at 6pm under the old oak tree.
Or meet the police at your house when you return from school.

Until then, best regards,
Someone who has proof of your love affair

He dropped the letter off like he had before. He just needed Ms. Hayes to be distracted, which was very easy to come by, and the letter was set in Ralph's mailbox, waiting to be picked up.

By lunch time, Sidney was prepped and ready for what was to come. His anger rose even more when they discovered that Abby was at the hospital due to complications from her abortion. Charlie asked to be by her side, which no one hesitated to stop. He was always a good guy to anyone and everyone. The school day came to an end more quickly than Sidney could have anticipated, and he watched as Ralph questioned poor Ms. Hayes about a mysterious note that he had. He watched from a distance as a shaken, visibly distressed Mr. Ralph Smithinson paced around the upper hallway, obviously deciding which fate he would rather face. Sidney began to wonder what he would do if Ralph didn't show up. Would he actually call the cops? Probably not. Nothing good ever came from trying to get the police involved in anything. He would just have to find another way to make him suffer if this plan didn't work.

After school, Sidney headed home to prepare. He had a quick bite to eat while Lucia got ready to head out. She planned on having dinner tonight with Bella, which would make it easier for Sidney to slip out unnoticed. Once Lucia had left, Sidney got himself changed into his hoodie and grabbed the bag the had packed the night before. The bag only contained two things - a slingshot and some rocks.

He was able to make his way back to the school at around 5:30pm. That gave him enough time for target practice and to begin the irritation of the nest. He set himself up around the side of the building, where he could hide away if he needed to, and he began to test for the perfect angle to hit the hive. His fifth shot successfully hit the hive, and he studied the movement, looking for any weaknesses in its structure. He watched more wasps emerge from the hive with each hit. His eleventh shot took out a decent chunk of the nest, and he could tell that the flying insects were very on edge. Pulling his phone from his pocket, he observed the time. It was ten to six. Replacing his phone in his pocket, he lined up rocks on the small ledge next to him.

Sidney's heart rate spiked when he

heard the door to the school, and he armed himself with his first rock. Leaning away from the edge of the building, he witnessed a nicely dressed Ralph Smithinson approach the area around the oak tree. Sidney lined up his shot and fired, clipping the top of the nest once more. He pressed his body flush against the wall, giving a moment, in case Ralph saw the flying rock. The only sound he heard was his racing heartbeat. Peering around once more, he laid eyes on Ralph, who stared off towards the road, the nest within ten feet of him. Sidney observed Ralph waving his hand around and pacing quite a bit. The wasps were definitely on guard. Sidney fired another shot and followed up with hiding, waiting for any sounds. He fired then, again... and again. Each time, Ralph was completely unaware of what was happening around him. More than likely, he was preoccupied with keeping his disgusting extracurricular a secret.

Ralph began to pace up and down the sidewalk, obviously growing impatient. The wasps were extremely active and agitated, and Sidney was now down to his last rock. Taking a deep breath, he said a prayer. Lucia always told him to pray when he wanted something, and if it was meant to be, then it would be granted. He waited for Ralph to turn his back, and as he paced down the sidewalk once more, Sidney took a deep breath and fired. The rock clipped what remained of the nest that kept it attached to the tree, which sent the nest plunging to the ground...

Right. Next. To. Ralph. An enraged hive swarmed around him. Sidney watched as Ralph began to flail his arms as the wasps swarmed him. Piercing screams escaped his throat as he struggled to escape. It was at that moment that Ralph tripped on one of the many rocks that Sidney had shot, sending him tumbling to the ground. Sidney stood there as the screaming continued for what seemed like an eternity.

When the screaming turned into a whimper and many of the wasps had left, Sidney emerged from the side of the building. With each step, his face twisted more and more into a sinister grin. Ralph laid on the ground, gasping for air, his body swelling everywhere that Sidney could see. Ralph caught a glimpse of Sidney out of the corner of his eyes and mouthed "help," but the only sound that escaped was a squeak. Sidney stopped just above his head. He was unrecognizable with the number of stings that covered his face. Ralph reached his arm up, but Sidney just threw his head back and let out a low, horrifying laugh. Ralph's arm fell back down to his side, and Sidney peered at him with those intense eyes, watching for any chest movement. He knew not to touch the body, and he began to pick up a good amount of the rocks and shove them in his bag. When Sidney was satisfied, he approached Ralph once more and gave him a quick tap with his foot. There was no movement coming from Ralph, but he did notice something sticking out from his shirt pocket. Sidney carefully reached down and pulled out the letter he had left for Ralph. That was one less thing that he would have to search for. Nodding his head in the direction of Ralph, a smile plastered his face as he said, "Thank you." The feeling of accomplishment and satisfaction rushed through Sidney as he walked away from the lifeless body of the dirt bag that was Mr. Ralph Smithinson.

But Sidney's entertainment was not going to end there today. As he rounded to the front of the building, he witnessed a young blonde girl drop a stack of books she held in her petite arms. Sidney rushed over to help her as she fumbled with the books, obviously embarrassed. They both stood in unison, locking eyes. Her cheeks were pink, and she had eyes that reminded him of the sky. He handed her what few books he was able to pick up as a genuine smile crossed her face and a soft voice spoke, "Thank you so much." Sidney stood there, speechless, as he stared at her. Her eyes were soft, and her smile reached her eyes, which glistened in what little light remained in the sky. "I'm Jenna," she said with a little hop, shifting her weight on and off the balls of her feet.

"S-Sidney," he said, wide-eyed like a deer in headlights.

Jenna gave a small chuckle as she placed her hand on his arm, "Thanks again." She slipped past him and headed on her way.

Sidney just stood there in awe. Her face, her voice - she was like an angel. She was kind, and she smiled at him. A genuine smile crossed Sidney's face as he looked down at his feet. Shoving his hands into his hoodie pocket, he started to head home with a grin plastered on his face as he remembered his accomplished mission. Just then, a sharp, deafening scream echoed through the parking lot behind him, the parking lot where Ralph's dead body laid... the direction that Jenna had gone...

CHAPTER ELEVEN

Jack leaned forward, resting his arm on the side of his chair. "What did you feel in that moment?"

Sid leaned in towards Jack, placing his hands on his knees. "It wasn't fear, if that is what you are asking. I have nothing to fear. In that moment, I felt I may have damaged someone innocent. It's not every day you find a dead body."

"Why do you say you 'may have?'"

"Jenna and I were woven from the same thread. Handed similar paths, she's my light and I, her darkness. When I first told her about everything, she thanked me." Sid chuckled as he leaned back into his chair. "She thanked me, when it should have been the other way around."

Jack made a notation in his notebook.

"Why did she thank you?"

"For telling her the truth, and..." Sid sighed, "for saving her, 'even though it cost a life,' she had said. I tried to get her to understand that Danny's life was worth nothing in comparison to hers. Deep down, she knew, though."

"She knew he was nothing?"

"No, that I was involved in his death. But at fourteen, who would think that someone your age is capable of murder?"

"Why do you call only some of your kills murders?" Jack scribbled in his notepad once more.

Sid shook his head at Jack. "You classify me as a murderer. I don't see it that way. As I have said before, my methods are unconventional, but they work. The system failed her once, I wasn't going to let him hurt her again."

⤜ ⤜ ⤜ ⤜ ⤜

A few months had passed since Ralph's death, and school seemed to get back to normal, except for the fact that Jenna had taken an interest in Sidney. He couldn't understand why, but she attached herself to him. Almost every day, they would hang out. Baseball had started, so that took up most of Andy's time. Charlie was helping his dad with the family business, and Lucia was working a bit more than normal. All-in-all, it was nice to have someone around.

Andy, Charlie, Abby, Jenna, and Sidney

became a close-knit group of friends. Andy liked to tease that he was the third wheel, but Sidney had no idea if Jenna even liked him like that. They talked and hung out like normal kids, but it wasn't until she called one night, in the middle of the night, that Sidney knew they were closer than just friends.

It was almost midnight when Sidney awoke to his phone ringing. He thought he had been dreaming but, sure enough, under his pillow, his phone was lit up with a missed call. Turns out, not just one missed call, but three, and over ten messages from Jenna. Sidney shot up from his bed, staring at his screen, reading over the messages. One said that Jenna was at the school. Why was she at the school at midnight? There were no details, only vague messages stating she needed some help and to not tell anyone else. Sidney flew out of bed, threw on sweats, and took off running towards the school without a second thought. He only hoped that Lucia wouldn't wake up and see him gone. Almost a block from school, he could see flashing lights. Once the school was in his sight, several cop cars came into view and panic rose for the first time, in a very long time. As he continued to run towards the police cars, an officer came into view, and he rose his arms to stop Sidney from coming any farther. "Where is she?" Sidney shouted at the officer, his breathing heavy.

"Son, you can't be here right now." The officer continued to block Sidney from getting any farther.

"Jenna, is she okay? I'm not leaving until I see her!" Sidney stared at the cop, his hands balling into fists. He was in no mood for this.

"What's your name?"

He gave a sigh, "Sidney."

The cop leaned his head to his radio and began talking with someone on the other end. Sidney's arms crossed over his chest as he continued to go back and forth on the radio. "Any day now."

"I can't let you through right now," the officer said plainly.

"Well, I'm not leaving." Sidney cocked his head to the side as his face twisted in irritation.

A few minutes passed as the cop and Sidney stared at one another, the cop's face blank, while Sidney's irritation was easily witnessed. Out of nowhere, the cop smiled. "Hello, Mrs. Collins. Thank you for coming."

Lucia's voice broke through the quiet night, "Sidney James!"

>+>>+>>+>>+>>+>

Sid sat on his bed, staring at the stark white walls of his room. Jack felt they had made a "breakthrough" today, as he called it. If their talks continued to go in the right direction, Jack may even be comfortable with a visitor. Sid longed to see Jenna and would say anything to make that happen, even if he had to talk about the killing of Danny Rivera. The only person he opened up to about the death of Danny was Jenna until now. Sid would just bide his time until his next session, hoping Jack would allow Jenna to come see him.

The only problem was going to be Nurse Tyler, who was on for his shift tonight. Tyler rubbed Sid the wrong way. He was your stereotypical douche: egotistical, hyper-masculine, and always seemed to have an issue with Sid. It had been the same every time Tyler worked, ever since his first manic episode. Sid didn't even remember it, but Tyler sure did. It was never his intention to hurt anyone in the facility. Tyler was just the unlucky person who was in the wrong place, at the wrong time, when Sid lost it. Working in this line of work, it had to have happened to him before. He wondered why Tyler took it so personally with this event, or maybe it was just Sid he had a problem with? Sid was honestly getting tired of Tyler and his attitude. One night, Sid got under Tyler's skin, and a fight ensued. Of course, Sid was blamed for it, but he had been planning a way to get back at him. Still no definite plan, but it was in the works.

Right on cue, Tyler appeared in Sid's window with his nauseating grin. "Sid, still awake, I see. No problems tonight, understand?"

Sid's eyes remained on the wall, his face expressionless, "Understood."

"What's the matter? Lonely in your cage, monster?" As always, Tyler was looking to get a reaction from Sid. He always insulted and attempted to belittle him, but when Sid didn't respond, it would piss him off. Tyler glanced around the hallway before leaning towards the door again. "That beautiful blonde of yours is probably lonely as well. Too bad she doesn't have a real man to take care of her."

Sid took a long, slow, deep breath before responding, "I wasn't aware that you were a man to begin with. You talk big game, probably to make up for the small size, due to all those steroids you take."

A door slammed down the hall, and Tyler's name was called. Tyler let out a grumble, glaring at Sid. "I'm more of a man than you will ever be, and I can visit Jenna to prove it."

"Tyler!" shouted another person, as Sid shot up out of bed, those piercing blue eyes glaring at Tyler.

"We got a live one!" Tyler shouted, turning his attention back to Sid, a heinous grin plastered across his face.

Nurse Amber appeared into view in the door window. "Everything okay here?"

"Everything is fine," Sid chimed in before Tyler. He knew Tyler's game by now. Without missing a beat, Sid stated, "I need to use the bathroom, and I asked for Tyler to not stare." A mischievous smile crossed Sid's face.

"That's-" Tyler started.

"Move on, Tyler, and finish your rounds," Amber said in an authoritative tone.

Sid sat back down on his bed with a sigh of relief as the nurses disappeared. Tonight was going to be a long night, if he couldn't fall asleep.

>+>+>+>+>+

The next day, Jenna was not at school. She wasn't responding to calls or messages, and no one in the group had heard from her. When Sidney explained to Lucia what happened, she wasn't upset anymore. She just wished he had woken her up to help. When Sidney told his friends what happened, everyone became on edge. Three days passed before Jenna returned to school, and nothing would be the same after that. Jenna was covered in bruises, and as the others pressed her, Sidney stood there in utter shock, pain coursing through his entire body, as Jenna dodged questions regarding what had happened.

"Guys, enough!" Sidney shouted in the hallway. The group of friends and those around at their lockers all turned in shock, the silence almost deafening. Sidney grabbed Jenna's hand and began pulling her down the hallway, away from everyone.

"Wh-where are we going?" Jenna's voice was low.

Sidney continued to pull her towards the rear of the school, "We're getting out of here." And just like that, they left out a rear door. Jenna began to walk next to Sidney, still holding his hand. He saw her open her mouth a few times out of the corner of his eye, but she closed it instead of speaking. "You don't need to tell me," he said plainly. "You don't need to relive whatever happened and, trust me, school isn't where you want to be." Their pace had slowed a bit as they walked down the sidewalk. Sidney turned his attention to her as he looked over the marks and bruises. A weak smile crossed her face before she moved closer to him and rested her head against his shoulder. They walked for over an hour around town before they arrived at Sidney's favorite park. He led her down a path that was hidden by brush at the back of the park.

"Where are we-"

"It's a surprise. Just trust me." He smiled widely as they locked eyes. A smile crossed her face, but, for the first time, it didn't reach her eyes. She was truly hurting on the inside. He could only pray she would open up to him so he could help her. Coming up on a small clearing in the trees, a wooden swing came into view. "I put this up a few years ago." Sidney had stopped walking, but Jenna continued to walk forward, glancing all around. "Lucia helped me plant the flowers. It became my safe haven from her abusive husband." Sidney's head lowered. It was the first time he had talked about Arthur since his death. When he looked up, Jenna was staring at him, pain twisted on her face.

"Oh, Sidney... I didn't know." Jenna took in a sharp breath.

Sidney approached her, taking her hands into his. "No one did, except for Charlie and Andy. I just need you to know, you're not alone." Jenna pulled him over to the swing, and they sat down together.

A few hours passed by as they talked. Sidney opened up about the treatment he faced from not only Arthur, but his birth mother, as well. Jenna opened up about her mother, Tammy, and the boyfriend, Danny, who they left behind, how he found them and came back with a vengeance. While they talked, Sidney sent a few messages back and forth with Lucia so she knew where they were. As always, she wasn't mad in the slightest. She understood and just asked to be kept in the loop. By the middle of the day, they headed for Sidney's house for food. Sidney promised Jenna that he would protect her, at any cost.

>|» >|» >|» >|» >|»

"His was the easiest death to plan," Sid said as he leaned back into his chair. "Jenna told me everything I needed to know, and he was dead before morning."

"Were you afraid that you would get caught? You went into the house in the middle of the night, with everyone there." Jack leaned forward.

"Jenna was not there. She slept at my house that night. Her mother never knew the difference, and I knew she would be safer with me. Lucia never protested. She knew she needed to be kept safe."

"You asked Lucia if she could stay the night?" Jack asked.

"Yes, and all it took was one look at the

bruises for Lucia to insist that she stay."

"With every murder-"

"Death," Sid interrupted.

Jack cocked his head to the side, "With every... death, did you notice anything changing?"

"I got a lot better at covering my tracks. I learned to not leave fingerprints, to wear a hat to cover my hair." Sid smiled. "Leaving any DNA or a trace of me would be careless. I have always been meticulous with everything in my life."

"Did Jenna ever question his death?"

"She had no idea that I killed him. When I said he was the easiest, I wasn't exaggerating. He was a druggie. When you are high and drunk, an overdose is a very possible outcome."

"What about Tammy?" Jack asked as he tapped his notebook.

"I contemplated ending her misery as well, but I had no idea what would happen to Jenna. If Tammy died, where would Jenna have ended up? Losing her, I didn't think I would be able to deal with that. We understood each other in a way that no one else could. I could only hope that with Danny gone, Tammy would attempt to get her life back on track. That was the whole reason they moved to Glenwood in the first place." Sid shrugged with a sigh. "I knew there was a chance that Tammy's ways wouldn't change, and I would have to help Jenna once more, but Tammy did turn around. Jenna doesn't have a lot to do with her, but she is clean and sober. Finding your boyfriend dead from an overdose can be a wonderful wake up call."

"So, with Jenna, you left her mother alive, giving her a second chance. Why wasn't it the same with Charlie's father, Hudson?" Jack shifted in his seat as he waited for an answer.

Sid's face twisted as he thought about Hudson Cooper. "The crimes he committed were unforgivable. The shame he brought, the number of people he hurt. He helped destroy thousands of lives..." Sid's fists balled up at the thought of it all. Taking a deep breath, he relaxed into his chair. "The information was getting out about his illegal practices. Their house was raided, and Charlie did not feel safe. Lucia and Hudson made plans for Charlie to stay the night, one day. She agreed to allowing Charlie to stay a few nights, not knowing that this arraignment was going to be made permanent. Charlie had a place to go, Jenna did not."

Jack rose from his seat, tucking his notepad under his arm. "That is enough for today."

Sid rose quickly, "Jack?!"

"Yes?"

"What about a visitor?" Sid took a deep breath.

"I will call Jenna in the morning and set it up for you. As long as there are no problems between now and then, you will see her in a couple days." Jack gave a quick nod towards Sid.

Sid sighed, "What if I am having an issue with someone on the staff?"

Jack's face twisted, concern crossing his face. "Are you having issues?"

Sid shook his head, "No, I-" Another sigh escaped his mouth. "I just want to see her."

Jack nodded, "Someday, I hope you will open up completely so we can work through all of this, but if something is happening, you can tell me. I do not tolerate mistreatment in my facility."

Sid and Jack just stared at one another for a few moments before Sid shook his head, "His name is Tyler. Just look into him, is all I ask." For the first time in his life, he was giving control over to someone else. If Tyler was to be punished, he would let the proper people handle it. That never felt more foreign to him.

CHAPTER TWELVE

The summer between middle school and high school brought on big changes, and some were not for the better. Sid and Jenna became inseparable, they were together almost every day. Lucia had a pool installed, so their house became the official hang out spot. There was only one person who seemed to be missing from the group hangouts. Charlie never seemed to answer his phone or messages. When he responded, the messages were brief. Most of the messages stated he was busy helping his father and he would get back to them later. There was only one problem with that, later never happened. If it wasn't for the occasional phone calls that lasted only a few minutes max, Sidney would've thought he was dead.

Some days, the group, excluding Charlie, hung out together. Other days, Jenna chased everyone off, saying she wasn't sharing that day. Lucia worked Monday through Friday and only asked for Sidney to spend one weekend day with her. Over the course of the summer, it turned into one weekend meal instead of an entire day. Lucia had even invited Tammy, Jenna's mother, over for dinner a few times, and they hit it off. Tammy had gotten herself on the right track and was clean and sober. Tammy, Lucia, and Bella had what they called "Girl Days," and Sidney would end up hanging out with Andy that day because Abby and Jenna usually joined in on the fun. Every couple of weeks, the boys were left alone to get into trouble, and trouble did happen. The first time, they ran off with some beer that they took without Lucia noticing. Andy and Sidney got drunk out by the football field but were not caught. The second time they stole beer, Andy attempted to roast some hot dogs and built a fire in the middle of the football field. They were busted less than thirty minutes later because of security cameras and the fun fact that there were still people in the school during the summer, a thought that never crossed the minds of two fifteen-year-olds. There was no third attempt at shenanigans because Lucia threatened to ground Sidney for the rest of the summer, which made Jenna threaten to kill him if he ruined the summer by doing stupid stuff.

Three weeks until the start of high

school, and Charlie had yet to hang out with his friends, but all that was going to change. As was done almost every day, Andy sent out a group text in the morning to find out who had what planned for the day. Weather called for a hot day, so the girls wanted to hang out at Sidney's by the pool. Sidney was in complete shock when Charlie responded to the message saying he would be there around eleven. Sidney headed down the stairs to give Lucia a heads up, when the smell of bacon hit his nose. As he entered the kitchen, Lucia smiled up at him, and Jenna was already sitting with a cup of tea at the far end of the table. "Sorry, I forgot," Sidney said as he plopped down in the chair beside Jenna. Tammy had gotten a job at a big box store in the next town over, as there were not many options in this small town, and usually dropped Jenna off here in the morning so she wouldn't have to be alone.

"It's okay, Lucia kept me company." Jenna smiled, leaning her head on Sidney's shoulder. Lifting her phone in front of his face, she continued. "You see this?" She must have been referencing to the message from Charlie because even he thought it was strange.

"Everything okay?" Lucia said, turning away from them to place a dish into the sink.

"Well, first off, this is a warning that everyone is coming over today," Sidney said as Jenna lowered her phone to the table.

Lucia let out a small laugh. "Figured as much, with how the weather forecast looked." She paused a moment. "So...?" she wiggled the tongs towards the two in the corner.

"Charlie," Sidney said plainly.

"You talked to him?" Lucia said, as she carried over a plate of bacon.

"He said he is coming over today after ghosting us all summer," Jenna said, slightly annoyed.

Sidney agreed with Jenna's feeling on the matter. It wasn't that they didn't want him here; he was their friend. It was the fact that he didn't talk to them all summer and kept his friends out of the loop.

"He's actually going to be staying the night," Lucia said nonchalantly, as she turned her back, heading back towards the counter. "For a few nights," she continued. Her shoulders shrugged. "Hud called this morning and asked if it was okay. I didn't see a problem in it, as the two of you haven't hung out much with him working at the warehouse with his dad." Sidney sat there dumbfounded; Jenna's mouth hung open as Lucia turned with a plate of pancakes. "What?"

"Not that I don't want to hang with Charlie, but doesn't that seem weird?" Sidney stuffed bacon in his mouth before continuing, his voice muffled by the food, "Haven't seen him all summer, and now he wants to chill?"

"Gross!" Jenna said as she hit Sidney in the shoulder.

Lucia gave a huff as she set the plate on the table. "I don't know the entire story. All I know is Charlie needs a safe place to stay for a couple days, and I offered because the Marshall's leave tomorrow to head to their cabin like they do at the end of every summer." She sat down in her seat and glanced between the two lovebirds before continuing, "Don't bother Charlie with a lot of questions. If he wants you to know, he will tell you."

The rest of breakfast was as normal as usual, with Jenna and Sidney side by side, and Lucia teasing them. Sidney had introduced Jenna to video games, and she loved to play with him. She always said that "it helped her feel closer to him." Lucia got a kick out of the two of them and their antics. By ten, Abby had arrived, so Sidney was ditched as the girls headed out to lie in the sun and gossip. He just continued to play on his gaming console while he waited for someone else to show up. Right before eleven, Andy came running in the house and tripped over the vacuum cord that Lucia was using. He was panting and trying to form words. Lucia stopped the vacuum as she attempted to listen closer to what Andy was saying. The only thing Sidney could make out was "TV" and "News." Lucia quickly scooped up the remote and tuned in to the news channel. There, plastered all over the TV, was none other than Hudson Cooper, Charlie's father. Before much of anything could come through the TV, Lucia flipped it off and said, "Outside, now."

"But..." Andy said.

Lucia just stared at him with "the look" and, without saying another word, Andy walked right out of the living room. Sidney stood to leave, but Lucia grabbed his arm.

"Do not pester Charlie about it, and do not let Andy, either." Sidney gave a nod, knowing he would respect Lucia's wishes, but that didn't stop his mind from wandering.

By the time Sidney was outside and reached the deck, Andy had already disclosed what little was known to the girls. Abby was first to jump up from her seat. "What did Lucia say?"

"What is going on?" Jenna followed up with.

Sidney just shook his head.

"No? No, what?" Abby said as she placed a hand on her hip.

"She said not to jump on Charlie when he gets here." That was all Sidney knew to say. He had no idea what was happening, but it wasn't good, that was for certain.

Jenna crossed her arms over her chest, her face still twisted in confusion. "Do you think she knows, though? I mean, she told us Charlie is coming to stay for a couple of days."

Andy's eyes got wide. "When was that?"

"This morning over breakfast," Jenna said with a small shrug. Her eyes wandered over to Sidney. Silence passed over the group for but a moment before Jenna spoke once more, "It was really Hud?"

Sidney nodded slowly. "And it was a mugshot. It wasn't like a normal picture."

"Poor Charlie," Abby said as her head lowered to the ground.

It was going to be hard to pretend they hadn't seen anything, but they were going to have to try their best. Not even a moment later, a voice came from the sliding glass door, "Hey, guys..." Four sets of eyes shot up, landing on Charlie, standing there awkwardly. This was going to be a lot harder than Sidney thought possible. The tension seemed so thick, but, thankfully, Lucia came to the rescue, bringing out a tray of snacks.

"There is more where this comes from, so eat up!" she shouted with a smile on her face, but her eyes told the true story.

He knew what that look meant. He put a half-fake smile on his face as he ran up and gave his best friend a bear hug. "Thank God you're here. We are finally tied with the girls for votes!" Sidney awkwardly let go and headed towards Lucia and the tray of food. "I was just saying that maybe we could order some pizza, but the girls wanted salads." Popping a piece of strawberry in his mouth, he glanced over to his friends. "Don't you think pizza sounds good, Charlie?"

Lucia gave Sidney a quick squeeze of approval on his shoulder before heading inside. Everyone's demeanor changed with the help of Sidney's antics. The five friends were able to hang out without another thought of Hudson Cooper. Lucia ordered pizza for everyone, given no choice with the escape that Sidney had concocted. It was a great day that passed all too quickly, leaving the night upon them with Charlie and Sidney alone. Now that it was just the two of them, awkwardness slowly crept between them.

"So..." Charlie said as he sat in the

chair across from Sidney.

Sidney's eyebrows raised in response. "Yeah?"

"How's the summer been going for you?"

"Is that really all you want to talk about?" Sidney's face contorted in irritation. "Where the hell have you been all summer?"

Leaning back into the chair, Charlie sighed. "Things got really hard down at the warehouse. My dad was super stressed, and I had to help. He didn't want me there at first, but then he changed his mind. It was nice working with him and helping with the family business."

"But...?" Sidney pushed himself off the wall and started to walk towards Charlie.

Charlie sat up, his back stiffening. "What do you know?"

"The only thing I saw was Hud's face briefly plastered all over the news." Sidney crossed his arms over his chest. He knew Lucia didn't want him to pry, but he couldn't just sit back and not do anything. It wasn't in Sidney's nature. If Charlie was in any trouble, he needed to help. Hud was a great guy, but if he had done anything to hurt Charlie... The silence seemed to echo off the walls in an almost deafening manor as Charlie and Sidney just stared at each other. He knew that if Hud had hurt Charlie, he may not want to open up about it, but that would mean that he couldn't help. One more time, he decided. He was going to press him one more time. "He didn't...?" Sidney said as he swung his arm between them, his voice trailing off.

Charlie's head shook slowly. "No, he didn't... what he did was so much worse, Sid." Charlie's head lowered, defeated. Whatever had happened really took its toll. He wasn't going to hassle him anymore. If he offered it up, that would be another story. Obviously, the news was already out, and it was a punishable offense. What would that mean for Charlie, though? His mother died of cancer only four years earlier so, without Hudson, Charlie would be alone in the world. No matter the outcome, Hudson would have to face the consequences of his actions and hope that the fallout would not affect Charlie negatively.

Almost a week had passed, and everyone was preparing for the start of freshman year. It was a big deal to many people, but both Charlie and Sidney had their minds preoccupied with other thoughts. Sidney was worried about Charlie. Hell, almost everyone was worried about him. Lucia was overheard talking to Tammy about how Charlie was handling everything and that it wasn't going well at all. Sidney had managed to keep his nose out of it, not that he had a chance to be nosy. Jenna was still over almost every day and, because of Charlie, Abby joined in. Andy wasn't going to be back until the Sunday before school started, so it was just the four of them.

The tip of the iceberg finally hit and sent a normally polite and kindhearted Charlie into a rage that no one had ever seen before. Charlie had been on the phone with his father when the screaming began. By the time Lucia made it outside to Charlie, several chairs were flipped, and his phone was smashed. Sidney knew he needed to help his friend. He couldn't continue to stand by and do nothing. He would give Charlie the night to calm down, and then Sidney would get answers. The next morning, Sidney sent a message to the girls letting them know that Charlie and Sidney were having a guy's day, hoping with just the two of them, Charlie would open up.

The day seemed to pass them by with no sign that Charlie was going to open up. The two boys stayed in the house, per Charlie's request. He never wanted to leave the house anymore, and that was more than likely because of the situation involving his father. Lucia offered to take the boys out to get new phones, but Charlie politely turned her down. After dinner, Sidney couldn't hold it in anymore. "Are you going to tell me, or do I need to look it up?" His arms were crossed over his chest, his eyes hard. "I've been trying to respect it like Lucia wanted but, dude, you need to talk to someone."

Charlie plopped himself down on the edge of his bed, his head buried into his hands. When he looked up at Sidney, pain flashed across his face. "It wouldn't be so bad if he hadn't blamed my mom. That is what is so fucked up. His excuses relate to my mom passing, as if it justified his actions."

Sidney took a step forward, placing his hand on his friend's shoulder. "What happened?"

Charlie started from the beginning, when things went downhill, when his mother got sick. What started out as a lump in her chest, spread to other areas so quickly. By the time the cancer was discovered, it was too late. That didn't stop Emily from fighting the fight. Surgeries and treatments proved to be unsuccessful. After four long months, Emily passed away, and Hudson was left, not only mourning the love of his life, but with thousands of dollars in medical bills. Rumors of their money troubles floated throughout town when Hudson wasn't able to get another loan from the bank. The whispers made it all the way to the closest city to the west and into the ears of a local gang, The North-side Gunners. The money they offered was too good to pass and, thus, a partnership was born. Hudson's pockets were lined with cash, and he turned a blind eye to what came through on the shipping containers. What started out as weapons quickly expanded into drugs. That was when the gang got really cocky, which would ultimately catch the feds' attention. Human trafficking would be the downfall of the entire operation that had been running for the past few years, and the gang had their fall guy, Hudson Cooper.

That night, Charlie and Sidney barely looked at one another. Sidney attempted to comfort his friend, but it backfired, making Charlie push him away. Sidney understood Charlie would need space, and he had business to take care of, anyways.

Hudson may not have completed the crimes himself, but like a coward, he turned a blind eye to the suffering around him. Sidney needed to dive deeper into Hudson's case to find out just how far down the rabbit hole the crimes went. Not only did he need to look up what Hudson was being charged with, he needed to backtrack and look at crimes that had been committed by The North-side Gunners. Sidney stayed up all night, and by the morning, he had seen enough to last him a lifetime. Hudson's crimes went a lot farther than turning a blind eye. Because of his actions, innocent lives had been lost. Nothing was worse than those who would have to continue to live with the trauma they faced, or the memories of the trauma they faced from the hands of The North-side Gunners. There was no redemption for a man like Hudson. Thousands of lives were ruined from his actions, not just his son's life. Hudson deserved everything that he had coming to him and so much more. He betrayed those around him and would come face to face with the ultimate betrayal by Sidney's hands.

CHAPTER
THIRTEEN

The next twenty-four hours blurred for Sidney, his actions seemingly not his own. By the following afternoon, it was all over the news. Hudson Cooper had been found murdered in his home when he did not show for a meeting that morning. Silence filled the house as everyone sat, surrounding the TV, taking in the news. Investigators were already on the scene, and whispers floated that it had been a gang related hit to keep Hudson from talking. The whispers stated Hudson was possibly meeting with the United States Attorney for a discussion of a plea deal. Everyone knew that a plea deal meant that Hudson would talk, and that is the last thing any gang would want to happen. Only the events played out a little differently than the police would ever know. There were only two people who knew the truth of last night, and only one of those people currently lived.

Charlie wanted space from everyone. Sidney understood and knew, eventually, he would come around. Lucia was already on the phone with multiple people, trying to figure out the next steps to take, because in her custody, was a now orphaned boy. Sidney knew that Lucia would never turn Charlie away and that he would have a safe home here. There was more than enough room, and Charlie was already family in his eyes.

Abby was the first to show up to the house, followed by Andy and Jenna, who arrived mere seconds behind one another. They all sat around the table, not much was passed around in the sense of words.

"He's really...?" Confusion crossed Abby's distressed features.

Lucia began to load up the table with snacks as she paced around the kitchen on the phone. "You do realize that this would leave two teenage boys in my care? Who even knows if he wants to stay here? How do I even begin...?"

With the silence, everyone looked toward the doorway to the living room. Charlie stood there, his face emotionless. Abby stood slowly, unsure of what to do, but concern was easily visible to anyone looking on. "Charlie?" She took a few steps towards him before he rushed to her, scooping her into his arms, his breathing harsh over the room that was as silent as a graveyard. Jenna squeezed Sidney's hand as the three that remained at the table exchanged glances.

Minutes seemed to pass slowly as Charlie continued to embrace Abby before Lucia broke the silence. "I know this doesn't seem like the right time, and I don't ever think there will be a right time, but there is an investigator on the way to speak to you."

Abby whipped around, anger expressed in her features. "They can't even give him..."

"Not with a murder, sweetheart." Lucia's head slowly shook.

Charlie grabbed Abby's hand and pulled her back to him. "I understand that I have to talk to them. I don't know much, as I haven't talked to him." His head shook slowly. "I just don't know what is going to happen to me now."

Lucia approached Charlie with open arms, and he gladly took her embrace. "You don't need to worry about that at all. I will take care of all those details, and you are more than welcome to stay."

❯❯ ❯❯ ❯❯ ❯❯ ❯❯

"There was just that one officer who tried to speak up, stating things weren't adding up. He was told to sit down, shut up, and take the win. Not only did I save them from a long and drawn-out trial, I saved them having to deal with prison. Charlie no longer had to worry about what would happen." Sid sat across from Jack, his back straight as a pin.

"You believe the cops were just rushing through the job?" Jack said.

Sid nodded slowly, "Why make the case more difficult than it had to be? Hudson was charged with heinous crimes for helping a gang, and then he winds up dead? Who would even think to look at the son's best friend when he had all that stacked against him?"

"But what about Abby?" Jack said as he leaned in towards Sid.

Sid's expression remained relaxed. "There was a moment that I thought I would have to make it so she didn't talk. She started to ask questions, as well. Her parents fixed that problem for me rather quickly."

"You never feared you would get caught?"

≫≫≫≫≫

An investigator came and went multiple times over the course of the next few days. Each time, a new person in the group of five was interviewed, after the investigator had received permission from a parent or guardian. It was the topic of discussion, not just among the group, but the town as well. The investigator who interviewed members of the group asked questions that put Sidney on edge. Some questions included when the last time they had seen or spoke to Hudson, as well as who had recently been to the house. Sidney began to wonder if cameras had caught his movements. Had he been reckless and rash? There was no doubt in his mind that Hudson deserved what he had received, but Sidney wondered what would happen if anyone found out the truth. So far, his actions he held as a secret all his own, but what would happen if they came to light?

That was when Charlie was taken into custody only four days after his father's murder. Within a few hours, Lucia had him released, and the lead investigator apologized on behalf of the entire department for the one investigator who had been causing commotion throughout the group. Sidney was able to relax when they stopped coming around. News reported that there were no leads in the case and that the investigators wholeheartedly believed it was gang related. Abby, on the other hand, continued to question it. Her speculations were brought up almost daily. She pointed out that Hudson was killed inside his home, which means he let whoever into the house. Not only was the murderer let into the house, Hudson had been shot with his own gun that Charlie said he kept for safety reasons. If Hudson was really going to roll on the gang, the last thing he would do would be to let them into his house. He wouldn't even open the door, he would have called the cops. Charlie ended up calling the investigator himself, asking if it was possible that the gang had nothing to do with it. He told the group that the investigator reassured him they were doing everything they could to tie up all the loose ends. They neither confirmed nor denied the possibility of an external source behind the murder.

Questions passed throughout the group, but Sidney kept himself in complete control around them. He began to question himself and wondered what he could do so that Abby would stop putting ideas into Charlie's head. Abby's parents were quick to take care of that, though. The Kelman family already had issues with Charlie and Abby hanging out after the pregnancy incident, but Hudson's crimes blew the top off of everything. Two days before freshman year, Abby's family up and moved, leaving everyone with little notice and Charlie heartbroken after everything he had gone through.

Life settled down by November of freshman year. Hudson's case went cold, and Charlie stopped asking questions, wanting to move on with his life. The case against the gang continued, due to a money trail that led back to them. However, it had little to no effect on the small town. Charlie, Sidney, and Lucia settled into a new routine with the three of them. Lucia was able to get guardianship over Charlie with no fight at all. Just like Sidney had thought, none of his family wanted to remove him from his friends, unless Charlie wanted to leave. It ultimately came down to him, and Charlie asked to stay. Lucia was not going to deny him the one comfort he had, familiarity. Charlie heard from Abby only a handful of times since she had moved, but if it bothered him, nobody ever noticed. He had learned to mask his emotions very well. Life seemed content, and the four teens continued to move on with their lives. Sidney kept his head down, knowing he came very close to getting caught on his last venture. It would be almost two years before Sidney would take another risk, and it would be a major turning point in all their lives.

⇉ ⇉ ⇉ ⇉ ⇉

Jack and Sid sat across from one another in a room that Sid had not seen in quite some time. Jack stood from his chair and headed towards the door as he spoke, "We have come so far that I figured today's session could be a positive reinforcement to continue our treatment." Sid perked up in his chair as Jack opened the door to reveal a blue eyed, blonde-haired angel, her expressions soft as she rushed into the room. Sid quickly raised from his chair, taking his girl into a long awaited and needed embrace. She smelled of happiness - honey and coconut - and reminded him of the world just outside his prison.

As they continued their embrace, Jack could be heard shuffling from the room, allowing the two of them to have some privacy. Jenna pulled herself from Sid's chest, tears spilling from her angelic eyes. As he wiped them away, a smile spread across his face. "Please, don't cry for me, love. My heart couldn't stand it." She

130

buried her head once again into his chest as he lowered them to the couch beside them.

Once Jenna regained her composure, the two of them talked as if no time had passed at all. She talked about life outside of the hospital, how Charlie and his new wife were expecting a baby. Jenna had an advancement at her job, which had allowed her to move out of their small apartment and the stuffy city. She reassured Sid that he would absolutely love the house she moved into. It had always been a dream of theirs to buy a house together, and it pained him to hear that she had done it without him. His facial expressions must have changed because Jenna began to console him. She swore up and down that it was their house, not just hers. She was even having a balcony put in off of the master bedroom, just like Sid had envisioned.

He watched in awe as her bright and bubbly personality radiated throughout the room, changing the feeling completely. Jenna asked about his treatment here in the facility. He assured her he was receiving the best care possible, except for Nurse Hard-Ass. Her demeanor completely changed as Sid discussed the issues he had with Nurse Tyler, how he had gotten in trouble and been blamed when someone, who should have been professional, instigated him. Jenna's features hardened as she listened to what Tyler had said about her. Noticing a shift, Sid took her hands into his. He did not want her to worry about something so trivial. No one in their right mind would retaliate outside of their job... would they?

The hour passed quicker than either of them had expected. Jack came back in, stating that they needed to say their goodbyes. He stood looking on as Jenna began to tear up. Sid took her into his arms once more. "Don't you worry yourself, angel. I will be better for you, for us." With a quick kiss, Jenna took her leave, with Jack following behind. Sid was taken back to his room, and he relished in the smell that still surrounded him, knowing it would not be there forever, only a short while.

By morning, he felt the loneliness smothering him. Her smell was long gone, the warmth of her embrace dissipated with every second that passed since her departure. Only the promise he made lingered. If he continued his treatment and got better in the eyes of the doctors, he would be able to see her again and, hopefully, be able to go home with her someday. Seeing her today had been a strong, positive reinforcement to continue his dealings with Jack. As much as he did not want to continue to discuss his past regressions, if it meant he could one day return to Jenna, he would continue. She was all he had left in this dark and dismal world. His next meeting with Jack would go a lot differently than he would have ever expected, though.

↦ ↦ ↦ ↦ ↦

Freshman year finally brought an interest for Andy, who always felt like the third wheel. Her name was Rachel Wilson, and she had been going to school with Andy since her family moved to town back in kindergarten. She had mostly kept to herself until she had an accident in front of the Marshall's store. That was what caught Andy's attention, and the rest was history.

During sophomore year, Charlie met Aria Tannen, who was new to the district. The two of them hit it off from the very beginning. Aria was a very outgoing girl and approached him to ask for help when she got lost in the school. Charlie, being the gentleman he was, walked her to her class, and from there, he was head-over-heels. The group began to feel whole once more.

Junior year flew up on the group quickly. With life settled, Charlie and Sidney became closer than ever, even beginning to refer to one another as brothers. Charlie never spoke of his father, only his mother. He would visit his mother every year on Mother's Day and her birthday to bring flowers, but he never did anything for his father. Lucia said there may have been some resentment and to not push Charlie. Sidney, on the other hand, was more than happy to not speak of Hudson ever again.

With junior year, came talks of futures and questions about where they saw themselves in five or more years. Sidney honestly could not see himself without Jenna. Jenna and Sidney were still inseparable. With a promise to be responsible, Jenna was allowed to stay the night. Tammy trusted her daughter, and Lucia trusted him. They made sure not to break that trust and would save night time for strictly sleeping. Weekends alone, on the other hand, were completely different. What started as the normal fooling around, as teenagers do, was slowly evolving into something more intimate between the two.

Andy, Charlie, and Sidney were all psyched for the first football game of the season. Even though Sidney was not much of an athlete, the other two boys ended up convincing him to give it a shot. Turns out, Sidney was a very good kicker. Andy and Charlie played a lot more than Sidney, but he was okay with that. For once, he was just happy to be a part of a team, even with Logan Reed as the team's quarterback. He was an amazingly great player, but he gave off major douche-bag vibes and annoyed the ever-loving shit out of Sidney.

Aria was a very athletic and school-spirited girl and ended up convincing the other two girls to join the cheer squad junior year with her. So, as the school year rolled in, the group of six hung out on and off the field. It was a new and positive type of energy that Sidney enjoyed, but unfortunately, it would only last until the homecoming dance.

⤞ ⤞ ⤞ ⤞ ⤞

"In today's session, I would like to discuss something a little different, if you don't mind," Jack said as he crossed one leg over the other.

Sid perked up in his chair, taken aback by the sudden shift in energy. "What did you have in mind, doc?"

"We have been meeting for thirteen months now, and you have opened up about quite a bit. We have had some setbacks..."

Sid interjected, "My psychotic 'Andy' episode, you mean?"

Jack nodded, "Correct, but you have grown to trust me, have you not?"

Sid relaxed back into his chair, "I wouldn't say 'trust.' You intrigue me, as I do you."

Shaking his head slowly, Jack continued, "That is not what I meant. I mean, you have been able to open up to me, to discuss issues so we can work through them, correct?"

Sid slowly nodded. "Yes, we have. Your point, Jack?"

With a sigh, Jack lowered his leg and leaned toward Sid. "You need to tell me *everything* so I can help you."

Sid chuckled, "I have been, as we work through my life."

"Not that, Sid." He shook his head slowly as he stood. Holding out a pen and paper, he continued to speak, "You can write it, or say it, and I will write it, but I need to know everything that happened with Nurse Tyler Bradford." Jacks face was hardened as Sid looked up at him. He would see the anger in his eyes, and in that moment, he realized Jenna must have spoken to him. The question was, did he trust him enough to open up?

CHAPTER FOURTEEN

Makaila Peterson, the beauty of Edgeway High. She was the envy of the female student body, coveted by the male, and was head cheerleader every year since moving to town. Her father, Howard Peterson, moved his family to town to take the job of the late Mr. Ralph Smithinson. He was a respectable, God fearing man, as was the same for his daughter. She was modest and proper, which made it ever more so odd when the playboy of the school, Logan, asked her to homecoming, and she said, "Yes." Logan never even attempted to hide his transgressions. He played girls, and yet, girls still fell at his feet. It blew Sidney's mind and annoyed him the way everyone worshiped him because he could throw a football. But, as long as he didn't actually hurt anyone, he decided it wasn't his business.

Homecoming game, the first big game of the season, was always played against the Baylor Bears. The Baylor Bears and the Edgeway Eagles played every homecoming game together going back over thirty years, which made the two amazing rivals, and this would be the first year that Sidney was not sitting in the stands. Previous years, he watched and cheered on the guys on the football team. This year, he was in on the action and would have an up-close view of the girls cheering, where Jenna would be.

The guys were prepped and ready, hyped up for the game as they huddled around one another for the team meeting. The coin toss was in favor of the Bears, so they would be kicking off to them. The Eagles got to pick which side they wanted in return. Warmed up with two minutes left to kick off, they went over strategy as the cheerleaders warmed up on the track adjacent. They broke apart with a roar as they headed to their spots on the field. As Sidney ran out to take his place, he glanced first at Jenna, who was screaming with excitement from the track, and next at Lucia, who stood with pride in the stands, all decked out in Eagle gear. She was never a football person, didn't see the point in the game with all the violence on the field, but she was always his biggest supporter. He remembered back to when he told Lucia he was going to try out for the football team...

"You need how much money?" Lucia said, mouth gaping, with eyes to match.

"Just a little under a hundred. I guess you have to have certain things to try out." Sidney leaned across the counter.

"And you are trying out for what, exactly?" Lucia said as she turned, spoon still in hand.

"Football."

Silence filled the room as a smile slowly crept across her face. A rich sound engulfed the room as Lucia broke out into laughter. Sidney just stood there, staring at her. "That is the funniest thing I've ever heard! What do you really need the money for?"

Sidney raised his eyebrows, "Foot... ball."

Leaning onto the counter across from him, she slid a plate of poppers between them. "You're serious? Did you lose a bet against Andy?"

Sidney just stared at Lucia, annoyance crossing his face. "No, I would like to try out and maybe spend some time with my friends. We only have two years left together."

Lucia picked up a popper, twirling it in her fingers. "I cannot believe you are so close to graduating. Seven years and look how much you've grown."

Sidney reached out, grabbing Lucia by the hand. "I can never thank you enough for giving me a home."

"You were the first child we kept, and I am so glad we did."

At the buzzer, the scoreboard read 27 to

14, in favor of the Eagles. The crowds cheered as the players celebrated among one another. The adrenaline that spread through Sidney's veins was a welcomed change, compared to how he had been feeling. It wasn't that he was unhappy, by any means. How could he be? His life with Lucia would be the envy of any teenager. She didn't hover or pester. They lived a very decent life, and Sidney never felt like he went without, even on things that were not considered essential. Having Charlie around made it less lonely, though. Before, growing up alone was, well, lonely. The topper on his cake called life was Jenna. Even at seventeen, he knew he wanted to spend the rest of his life with her. She made everything better; she dulled the pain that Sidney felt. He couldn't see a life without her in it. So, what was wrong with his life? It had become boring, as it had fallen into a routine. Routine was not something that Sidney was used to, and it made life seem mundane. Football helped bring back some of the missing excitement. But how long would it last?

With the night coming to an end, a sweat-soaked Sidney ran up behind Jenna, pulling her into a musty bear hug. "Ugh! Gross! Sidney... stop!" she shrieked as he spun her around. With a chuckle, he set her back on the ground. Her face twisted as she turned to him. "You need a shower, desperately!"

With an arrogant, shit-eating grin plastered across his face, he responded, "Join me?"

"Over my dead body," came Lucia from

behind him.

"Busted!" shouted Charlie as he emerged from the doors to the locker room. Jenna was laughing hysterically as the group of friends slowly appeared.

"Everyone is still spending the night, though?" Sidney said as he wrapped an arm around Jenna, her face still beet red.

"If everyone behaves, yes," Lucia said sternly, with a hand on her hip, as she glared up at Sidney.

"Please, for the love of everything, shower!" Jenna said as she twisted away from him.

Aria came running up to the side of Jenna and grabbed her in the crook of her elbow, helping her make the daring escape from the stench that was a teenage boy. With a laugh, the group separated and headed into their respective locker rooms.

The night was filled with fun and laughter as they huddled around a fire pit in Sidney's backyard, roasting marshmallows and hot dogs, swimming in the pool that was lit up with colorful lights, and camping under the stars. For them, life was going to fly by, and harsh realities would drastically affect the group within the next few months. They just didn't know that yet, so in blissful ignorance, they continued to enjoy what youth they had left.

The next day, the boys lounged around Sidney's house while the girls headed out after brunch to get ready for the dance. Sidney thought that their rituals were ridiculous, but it made Jenna happy. Plus, it gave the guys some alone time. Andy felt smothered and was looking forward to a break from Rachel. Charlie, like Sidney, had no qualms about the girls being around. The day consisted of video games and junk food for the three boys, while Jenna checked in with each stop: nails, facials, hair, and make-up. They would make a pit stop at Aria's house before meeting the guys at the school.

The dance was already in full swing by the time the girls finally arrived. The guys had no idea how long they had been standing outside, as Andy had a football in his car that kept the boys occupied while they waited. The girls strolled up looking like they just walked out of a fashion magazine. Like every time before, when Jenna approached Sidney and gave him a kiss, he was awestruck. How could someone so beautiful and compassionate be with someone like him? If only she knew the truth, she would run screaming for the hills.

"Sidney?" Jenna said, pulling him back to reality. Her hand was held out to him. "Let's head inside."

Without a second of hesitation, he took her hand into his, and they headed into the building. Homecoming court was announced shortly after they had arrived, with Jenna, Aria, and Charlie on the court. Homecoming king and queen were none other than Edgeway High's power couple, Logan and Makaila. Charlie knew that teasing and jokes were going to ensue from his nomination into the homecoming court. Andy and Sidney sure did not miss a beat when it came to it.

"Make way for the prince!" shouted Andy as they moved through the cafeteria to get snacks.

Reaching the tables, Sidney held out a drink to Charlie with a smirk on his face. Charlie took the drink and shook his head, "I don't drink tea, it's nasty."

With a straight face, Sidney picked up another bottle and turned to Charlie, "But, it's his majes-tea."

The jokes were never ending, but it felt amazing to Sidney to have a night full of fun and laughter. The night took an unexpected turn when Rachel approached and asked the other girls for help. From over the loud music, Sidney only caught part of the conversation: Makaila, bathroom, crying. It didn't surprise him one bit because Logan was a pig. However, Charlie convinced Andy and Sidney to head out to the hallway to be backup for the girls, just in case his royal shit-stain decided to make an appearance and ruin anyone else's evening. They waited as guards, conversing among themselves for almost an hour, before the girls emerged from the bathroom. The boys were told to head home, as the girls were going to make sure Makaila made it home safely, and they would meet them back at Sidney's. With that, the three girls led a puffy-eyed Makaila from the school. By the time the girls returned to Sidney's house, the boys had already fallen asleep in the living room, with a movie still going on the television.

When morning came, Sidney figured they would hear all about what had happened, but the girls were quiet. Lucia even noticed the awkward quietness coming from the girls.

"So, how was the dance?" Lucia flipped a piece of French toast.

"It was fun," Aria chimed in.

The girls nodded enthusiastically, agreeing with the sentiment that Aria had said.

"Charlie is royalty!" Andy said as he stuffed his mouth.

"And that right there," Rachel said, pointing her fork at him, "is why you are not."

Andy smiled a big goofy smile as syrup ran down his chin.

Sidney was still curious about what happened with Makaila, so he knew he would have to bring it up. The other two wanted nothing to do with it. "And of course, Logan and Makaila were crowned king and queen. Just too bad what happened..."

Lucia turned rather quickly, her facial expression questionable. "What happened?"

Jenna kicked Sidney under the table while glaring him down. "Ow!"

Lucia set down the spatula and placed both palms on the counter. "What happened?"

"Logan's a pig, first of all," Rachel said, starting the long-awaited conversation.

"He made a move on Makaila, said she owed him," Aria continued.

Lucia placed a hand on her hip. "Owed him?"

"You know," Jenna said, eyebrows

raised.

"Oh..." Lucia turned away awkwardly.

"Why did she owe him?" Andy interjected.

"Because he supposedly made her, gave her the popularity she has, said she was nothing without him," Rachel said, turning towards Andy a bit.

Aria continued, "When she refused his advances, he broke it off with her."

Jenna shook her head slowly, "Poor girl was devastated, but we helped cheer her up the best we could, told her no good man would make her give herself up to him as if she was a prize."

"You hear that, Charlie?" Andy said, giving him a nudge.

Charlie turned to him, confused, with a mouth full of food. "What?"

Andy continued, a smirk crossing his face, "Now we know what's wrong with Sidney."

Sidney picked up a piece of bacon and chucked it at Andy. Laughs were passed around, and the energy in the room seemed to lighten, as did Jenna's posture. She seemed so tightly wound as they talked about the Makaila situation, and only Sidney knew why. He always hated what had happened to her growing up, but there was no way he could fix it. All he could do was be here for her now and help her through her tough times.

When Monday morning came around for school, the girls had made a plan to meet Makaila at the school to walk her in, if she wanted. It was the whole "girl solidarity" thing, and Andy said he didn't understand it. The group of six stood out front, waiting for Makaila, but did not expect what happened next. In pulls Ass-hat with his douche-mobile, but out from the passenger seat came none other than Makaila. The boys stood back and watched as the girls looked among themselves and whispered. Maybe it wasn't as bad as the girls made it out to be, but whatever had happened, Logan and Makaila had worked it out. Sidney grabbed Jenna by her elbow, encouraging her to come into the school with him. He figured she could talk to him if she felt she needed to, but she was eerily quiet the rest of the day.

Over the next few weeks, Jenna kept her distance with Makaila, even when the other two hung around her. Sidney always wondered if there was more to the story of what happened that night, but he would never press Jenna. If she wanted to talk, she knew Sidney was always there. There was just something about the night that just didn't go over well for her, and he figured it was from her personal past. She had her own secrets that she preferred to keep buried and only told minor details, or was very vague, in the general sense. Sidney learned quickly when the two started talking that Jenna would open up in her own time, and like Sidney, she had faced trials that no child should have to face. Jenna and Sidney were one in the same when it came to childhood trauma, though they both wore it differently.

Things slowly seemed to progress back to some sort of normalcy. The girls, including Jenna, hung out more, and when springtime rolled around, the four girls went prom dress shopping together. Junior prom was the highlight of Junior year, and what the girls had been impatiently waiting for. It was meant to be a night of fun and glamour. If the boys thought the girls went overboard for homecoming, they were in for an enormous surprise for prom. Jenna had all the details planned, everything had to match between her and Sidney. She tried to go as far as to make underwear match, but Sidney drew the line there. No one was going to see his underwear. Andy and Charlie both told of similar horror stories with Rachel and Aria. The girls even dragged the boys into helping make campaign posters for Aria to run for prom queen, which meant she was dragging Charlie into running for prom king. She didn't think they were going to win, but she still wanted to try.

The night before prom, everything was in place. Dresses and tuxes were ready to go, corsages were set in the fridge, awaiting to be placed upon wrists, the limo was set to bring them to and from the city where the venue was, and plans for the after party at a classmate's house were set in stone. Rachel kept repeating that this was going to be the best night of their lives. If only she knew that tomorrow night's events would lead several classmates down a dark path...

Her dress was ripped...
Blood and dirt stained her beautiful
pink gown...
Tears streaked the makeup, and dirt
marked her face...
Her screams of pure agony echoed as
she stumbled across the lawn...

"Don't forget the pictures!" Tammy shouted, as she ran out towards the group, as they headed towards the limo.

"Mom, don't you think you have enough?" Jenna laughed, waving her mother off.

"There will never be enough pictures of you," Sidney said as he took her hand into his. He placed his lips gently on her knuckles, giving a light kiss.

Andy scoffed, "Gross."

Rachel gave him a light punch as the group assembled themselves in front of the limo for a few more pictures.

All the parents gathered around the group once more as they took pictures, smiling, hoping to capture the magic of tonight, pictures that would last forever and would bring joy for years to come.

Aria's gown had black lace around the top, morphing into a dark green dress with a knee-high slit. Charlie matched with a green tux and black shirt. Andy, on the other hand, preferred a plainer look, as he chose a basic black tux. Rachel wore a beautiful tan halter dress with golden sparkles covering the skirt. Jenna, although not normally a pink person, chose a deep pink dress that dropped low in the back with a gem covered chain leading from the center of the shoulders, down the spine. Sidney had no taste and had left it up to Jenna what he would wear, which ended up being a simple black tux with a deep pink shirt to match.

Each girl shined in their own way, but in Sidney's eyes, nobody compared to Jenna. Maybe he was biased, but it didn't matter. He would have the most beautiful girl on his arm for prom, and if he had his way, the rest of their lives.

Prom was everything and more than Sidney could ever dream. The food, the decorations - everything was perfect. They danced the night away and ate some of the most delicious food he ever tasted. Prom king and queen came as no surprise when Logan and Makaila's names were called, but it didn't put a damper on anyone's evening. When prom ended, the high of the night still coated them, so to the after party they went.

The night continued with dramatic flair as they partied outdoors under the stars, but only an hour into the after party, the mood changed. Aria was the first to notice something was off, pulling Charlie's attention from the rest of the group, a figure stumbling from the woods in a dress. Aria took off running towards the figure, and Charlie followed close behind. Sidney caught a glimpse of Aria and headed in the same direction as the others. The closer they got, the more they could make out. It was a girl in a pink dress. The dress was ripped across the chest, and strips were ripped along the side and mid-line. From farther away, the dress looked dirty, but closer, Sidney could see that some of the streaks were blood. Makaila looked up at them, tears running down her cheeks, smearing the makeup and dirt on her face. Jenna approached from behind Sidney but froze in place when Makaila let out an antagonizing scream, falling to the ground. Her body sobbed uncontrollably as Aria attempted to cover Makaila with Charlie's jacket. There was no denying what had happened. Sidney looked at Andy, who caught Charlie's attention.

"Find him!" Charlie said with a hiss. Jenna was fumbling with her phone, but Rachel managed to dial the emergency number before grabbing her hand. The three boys took off and headed into the woods, splitting up only a short distance in, in an attempt to find Logan. Logan would not get away with what he had just done. Unlucky for him, Sidney would be the one that would find him. Sidney stalked up behind Logan, who was leaning against a broken railing at the edge of the bluffs. Stepping on a branch caused Logan to spin around, and they laid eyes on one another.

Logan looked confused, tears just barely appearing in the corners of his eyes. "I-I don't know what happened..." He looked down at his hands, which were shaking.

"What happened is that you are a sleazebag who can't take no for an answer!" Sidney's fist clenched as he continued to take steps towards Logan. He knew he needed to remain in control and not lash out. There was a possibility of witnesses, and he wasn't going to cross that line. He just needed to keep telling himself that.

"I didn't mean to hurt her!" Logan said, his voice pleading.

Sidney pulled out his phone. He didn't want to hear anymore. Letting the others know where they were would allow for him to have some backup. At least, that was his plan, until a message popped up from Jenna that read:

"He raped her."

The anger pierced him straight to his core. "You didn't mean to hurt her?" He slowly slid his phone back into his pocket, calculating his next moves carefully.

"It was an accident! I swear!" The pleading in Logan's voice twisted Sidney's insides even more.

Sidney put his hands up, defensively. "I completely understand." He stopped right in front of Logan. "An accident."

Logan let out a huff of relief, and Sidney watched as his expression changed. His face was now plastered with a shit-eating grin. "I'm glad you understand. You know how girls can be."

Sidney nodded slowly, a sinister smile crossing his face. "An accident, that is what everyone will say."

Logan's smile widened, his hand resting on Sidney's shoulder. "I'm glad you have my back."

"Such a sad accident..." With one swift movement, Sidney gripped Logan's tux with a vice grip and hurled him backwards. Logan had no time to respond. In a matter of seconds, Logan's body was sent hurtling over the railing and down the side of the bluffs into the darkness below.

CHAPTER FIFTEEN

"So, how did the conversation go?" Jack said.

"I sent a message to Charlie stating I found him. When he asked where, I told him. Then, less than thirty seconds later, I told him he jumped." Sid shrugged. "It was as simple as that."

Jack tapped lightly on the edge of his notebook. "No one questioned the situation?"

Sid shook his head, "Why would they? You have a girl accusing the star quarterback of rape, and he knows he got caught, that there is no escape. It wasn't like he could say that she agreed to it, he knocked her around." He gave another shrug before continuing, "Desperate times call for desperate measures."

"But taking his own life?" Jack said quizzically.

"The mindset was that his life was over. At seventeen, they can try you as an adult. Andy even said that he had to have known that that was the end of life as he knew it." Sid leaned back in his chair.

"You acted rashly when it came to killing Logan, don't you think?"

"I was overcome with rage, knowing that he could walk away that night. You already know how I feel about law enforcement and all that in general. I couldn't just let him do that and walk away. Even if they charged him, would he take a plea deal because of who his parents know? What if he didn't take the plea deal? Would Makaila drop the charges or be forced to face him in court? Could you imagine him walking away after what he did to her, having his freedom and living life as if he didn't hurt someone?" Sid leaned forward slowly, resting his hands on his knees. "I assessed the situation quickly, analyzed everything, and figured the quickest and cleanest way to take care of something like that."

"Did you ever question whether or not the fall would kill him?"

Sid shook his head quickly, "No. The ledge we were at, I remembered it from the many times I had been there myself. That ledge was almost a dead drop. If the drop didn't kill him, the waves and the force of the water on the rocks would have. Either way, the world would be free from one less despicable human being."

The night swallowed them whole. A police presence, parents rushing to the scene, looking for answers. All the while, a bunch of teenagers were attempting to come to terms about what had happened. Not just the death of a classmate, but the life-changing event that another had faced. Makaila had been taken to the hospital almost immediately after the first responders arrived. They had not known yet that there was a body either laying on the rocks below the bluff or floating in the lake. It all depended on how his body bounced on the way down. Sidney let Charlie tell the police what happened while he just looked on and, thus, began their rescue efforts, which would be proven futile within the first hour. There were over thirty students at this party, which made statements take a lot longer than most had wanted. Every student had to wait for a parent, and those who weren't directly involved with the night's events, were sent home and told to come down to the station the following day. As for Sidney's group, they had to stick around.

"Jesus Christ! This is taking forever! What more is there to ask?" Andy threw his arms up in the air, while hopping back onto the porch.

"Watch your language, son," Mike Marshall, Andy's father, said from behind them.

"But, seriously?" Rachel said, grabbing Andy's arm. "Don't they just need to talk to Sidney?" Sidney's head whipped around, glaring in Rachel's direction. "No offense!" she quickly added.

Jenna lifted her head off of Sidney's lap, pulling his attention back to her. "I'm not going anywhere." She gave him a soft smile. "I won't leave you to deal with this alone."

"Same," Charlie chimed in.

Aria nodded in acknowledgment. "We have your back."

Jenna shook her head slowly, bringing his hands into her own. "I cannot imagine what you are going through right now, seeing something like that."

"There was no denying he was guilty, seeing as he jumped," Aria said, irritation crossing her voice, which mimicked her facial expressions.

"Not everyone is equipped to deal with consequences of their actions. You lot are still very young and have a lot to learn," Julia, Aria's mother, chimed in. "I think I can speak for all of us adults here when I say, just talk to us."

"No matter what," Sidney started to say, but he became distracted by a visibly upset Jenna. He cupped his hand under her chin, and she relaxed, allowing her face to fall into him. He turned a bit to face his friends, still holding onto Jenna, before continuing, "Tonight, lives changed. It wasn't the night we all planned, but we helped a classmate in need, the best we could." He paused a moment, slowly making eye contact with his friends. "The other was... too far gone to help." It wasn't very hard for him to attempt to show compassion towards Logan, who definitely didn't deserve it. He needed to make sure to cover his tracks, and this was one of the best ways to do it. Turning back towards Jenna, he gave her a smile. "We will all have to deal with what happened tonight, on our own terms. But I know, if needed, I have ears around me that are open to listen, if I feel the need that I have to talk to someone." Jenna nodded slowly, some form of comfort she finally felt. He didn't understand why she seemed so concerned for him, when it was him who was worried of the impact on her, with what she had faced. Her past, like so many others, affected her life drastically, in both positive and negative ways.

It wasn't long before an officer approached, apologizing to everyone. Everyone was free to head home, but they may need to talk to some of us over the next few days. Sidney knew still, there could be a chance. Would the Reed family push for an investigation, or attempt to sweep the shame under the rug? There was no denying what had happened to Makaila, but these next few days would leave Sidney in a limbo, not knowing what was to come.

≫⊷ ≫⊷ ≫⊷ ≫⊷ ≫⊷

"They obviously never pushed for any

investigation, especially when the Peterson family came forward with an update on Makaila's condition." Sid took a sip of the coffee Jack had placed before him. He was beginning to enjoy the sessions.

"How bad was it?" Jack asked.

"She had two broken ribs, a broken wrist, with a few fingers that were dislocated on that same side, as well as the tearing from the assault itself. Dozens of bruises covered her body, Jenna had told me." His head shook and lowered a bit as he recalled the conversation with Jenna. "She was never the same, and she never returned to school. Who could blame her?"

"She wasn't the only one that didn't return, correct?" Jack leaned onto the table.

Sid just shook his head, "No."

"We will have to talk about him more, and I understand your hesitation. We do not have to discuss him at this point in time, but we will have to, eventually."

"You have said that I have come so far. I don't want to lose myself... like before." Sid twisted the cup around in his hands, his eyes sharp as he stared at Jack.

"Before, I don't believe you were ready to come to terms with his death. You weren't ready to admit what had happened. We don't have to discuss what happened in Trenmont City, but I want to continue following the sequence of events as they happened. So, what happened after prom?" Jack crossed one hand over the other, mimicking the energy that Sid had put out.

"Andy... he left Glenwood. Never said anything to anyone, not even his parents."

⪢ ⪢ ⪢ ⪢ ⪢

That following Monday, school was closed. The superintendent put out an email to all students and staff. The school would be closed Monday and Tuesday, due to the events that transpired over the weekend, and would reopen on Wednesday. There were crisis counselors for anyone who needed them. Lucia personally received a phone call from the school guidance counselor, asking if they needed anything and how Sidney was acting. Lucia and Sidney sat down after her phone call on Monday to talk about what had happened.

"You know you can talk to me."

"I know I can," Sidney said, annoyance crossing his face, "but I don't have anything to talk about."

"What happened with Logan..."

Sidney hit the table with closed fists. "What happened is he is scum. He thought he could put his hands on someone and not have any consequences."

Lucia and Sidney sat across from one another as the silence passed between them. Sidney relaxed, and she spoke once more, this time in a softer tone. "Just know that I won't judge you if you need to talk to me, and anything you tell me, stays between us." With that, she left the room,

159

leaving Sidney to think.

Texts were sent throughout the group of friends over the course of days while school was closed. Everyone's parents preferred that their perspective child stayed home. The messages proved that the parents were worried about what happened the night of prom and were now going to hover more than anyone liked. The kids voiced their distaste but had no choice but to stay home with their families. The group ended up making plans to meet up Wednesday before school, but there would be a slight change of plans.

Rachel came running up from behind the school, her arms waving as she hollered out to get everyone's attention, "Guys!"

All heads snapped in the direction of Rachel, who stopped just short of them, out of breath. "Andy- he..." She gave a huff before taking in a deep breath. "Andy, he's gone."

"What do you mean 'he's gone?!'" Charlie shouted, almost lunging at Rachel.

"Not like dead! Jeez!" She put her hands on her hips, defensively. "He left a note for his parents before sending me a message this morning. He hopped town; he's not coming back." Reaching into her pocket, she pulled out her phone and began to read...

I'm sorry, Rach, but I can't do this anymore.
I care for you very much.
You need to know that you did nothing wrong.
I can't continue to live in this town.
Glenwood isn't the town it used to be.
It is a black hole.
I am turning off my phone for now, as I don't want to be found.
Get out before it ruins you, too.
I am truly sorry.

The group just stood around, looking amongst each other. No words were exchanged, each person individually attempting to deal with this major change. At that moment, Sidney felt regret for the first time in his life. He felt that he had missed the signs that one of his closest friends needed his help, not realizing that it was his actions that had made Andy flee in the first place.

>+ >+> >+ >+> >+

Jack sat back down and slid another cup of coffee to Sid. "Did you ever realize that you were the reason he felt the need to flee?"

"I see it now, but back then, I didn't realize it." Sid took a sip from his cup.

"Would you change anything, knowing what you know now?"

161

"No." He sat watching the steam rise from his cup.

A few moments of silence passed between them. He could see Jack swaying from side to side, and the concern could be heard in Jack's voice when he spoke again, "Sid?"

He looked up at Jack. "I'm still here." He gave a sigh. "It is unfortunate, what happened to Andy, but we are all responsible for the choices we make. He didn't have to flee. He had friends and family who cared about him." Sid tapped his fingers against his cup. "Would I have told him the truth, had he confided his feelings to me?" He paused, taking a sip once more of his coffee before continuing, "No, but I would have attempted to make him see they did not deserve the air that was being wasted on them."

"Did you expect Lucia to respond the same way?"

"Never once did I expect that Lucia would try to leave Glenwood. She had said on multiple occasions that she did not want to uproot me. When she sat Charlie and I down to talk about it, I honestly expected Charlie to take her side, but he wanted to stay as well. This had not only been his family home, but he said he needed to restore his family name from the shame his father had put on it." Sid spun the cup around on the table, letting out a light chuckle. "I think it was that moment that she started to suspect that I wasn't entirely truthful with her. It would be years before she would tell me she knew, but it was after prom when she changed the way she was around me."

Jack leaned back into his chair, crossing his legs. "She started to treat you differently?"

Sid nodded, "She would tiptoe around certain subjects, especially those that pertained to that of a criminal nature. She insisted that we all go to counseling, to make for certain that everything was okay. The counselor I had asked me about how I felt about those around me, and if I felt safe or felt that I needed to make myself or anyone safe. Weird questions, that took me a while to catch onto."

"But you never confronted Lucia about it?"

Sid's head shook slowly as he stared down at his now empty cup. "Why would I? I honestly didn't think she knew. I didn't realize how much digging she had done without me knowing."

≫ ≫ ≫ ≫ ≫

The rest of junior year flew by, and the group grew even closer as the months passed. One of the parents suggested that the kids should get summer jobs. Thus, more parents pushed for it. When the summer hit, the group was only able to hang out a handful of times, but Jenna, she spent the night at Sidney's more than Tammy or Lucia expected. They acted mature, though, so it didn't seem to be a problem. They would get up for work and were managing their responsibilities like adults. Jenna and Sidney both decided to save their money, and whatever they earned was stuffed into a shoebox that Jenna had duck taped shut, with just a small slit in the top. Across the top in big, black letters was written *"**Our Getaway Fund**."* It was meant for after high school, for them to have some money to be together, no matter what colleges they ended up in.

College acceptance letters started to roll in, but no one opened any of the envelopes. One hot night in August, the group gathered all together for the first time that summer, to find out where their lives were going to lead them next year.

Aria and Charlie both got into the local community college in the neighboring city. Charlie was still adamant about staying in Glenwood and fixing his family name. Once he graduated, he was going to go to school for business and, hopefully, fix what his father had ruined. His father's company was currently being run by the board, with the hopes to hand it over to Charlie when he was ready.

Aria planned to help him and had applied to business programs, as well. Aria was a huge baker and had taken the classes that were offered at the high school. She wanted to open up her own business someday, but needed to have some knowledge of how to run a business. They were happy that they were going to be able to start the next chapter of their lives together. Aria hoped that she could help him rebuild his father's business and re-brand it into something more. They had goals that involved one another, and the happiness that radiated from them was infectious.

Rachel, on the other hand, decided she was leaving for college. She didn't care where, as long as she got into med school. Rachel was smart, and everyone knew that anything she set her mind to, she could accomplish. She had been through a lot throughout her time living in Glenwood, and Andy leaving really messed her up. She had still not heard from Andy, but his parents had heard he was safe where he was. Rachel was accepted into a state college on the other side of the country. She would be over twelve hours away, but she was excited to start a new journey. She insisted that they would forever be friends, but deep down, everyone knew that she needed a fresh start, and this just might be their last year together as friends.

Jenna was always interested in becoming a pharmacist. She wanted to start out small and make sure it was truly what she wanted to do, before committing her life to it. She had been accepted to a school in Trenmont City for the pharmacy tech program.

Sidney had also been accepted to the school in Trenmont City. He planned to obtain an accounting degree, with the hopes of working for himself someday. He had started to look for internships and what they entailed, in the hopes of landing one with a major company, to get himself a rep.

Jenna and Sidney were excited to be

able to continue their lives together. The money that they had saved would help them get established after they graduated from college. They agreed together, they would continue to save money. He hoped he could give Jenna the life she deserved.

Senior year started with hype. The girls stuck like glue, including doing cheerleading once more. Charlie convinced Sid that the football team needed them, and Sidney didn't want to disappoint his friend. This would be the last season they would play together. The group was enjoying whatever time they had left with one another. Homecoming came and went, which left Charlie and Rachel being crowned homecoming king and queen. Senior dinner dance appeared out of nowhere, leaving just a month left of senior year, a month of life as they knew it. Just one month until graduation.

CHAPTER SIXTEEN

Sidney stood, the black cap just at the edge of his fingertips, the world around him muffled, moving slowly. It was Jenna who brought him back to reality, as she had done many times before. She gripped his arm, her smile bright and just as warm as her touch, as she screamed over the cheering that now came in at full volume. "WE DID IT! AH!" Her happiness was so intoxicating and infectious. He opened his arms to her just in time, as she jumped up onto him, wrapping her arms around him. Today was a day to celebrate. Today, they were high schoolers no more. Everything that they had done, every event that happened, had brought them here to this day. If you had asked the eight-year-old Sidney, who sat in the police station the day his life changed, where he saw himself ten years from now, the last place he would have said would be at his graduation. In just two short months, Jenna and Sidney would be taking a road trip and beginning their lives outside of Glenwood. The joy he felt was almost overwhelming. He had been trying to be a better man for her, doing the best he could to keep his nose out of other people's dealings. So far, he had been successful, but how long would that last?

They partied the night away in Sidney's back yard. Full access to a pool made it the go to party spot for after graduation. Several other classmates chipped in and either bought, rented, or chipped in monetarily to make this the best party ever. Sidney's yard was transformed into a mini theme park with inflatable activities, including a giant bounce house, and food trucks. It was to be one last hurrah, before the reality of becoming adults was to set in.

Three weeks later, Sidney looked on from the driveway as Jenna loaded her last bag, Tammy hovering over her, asking a million questions, obviously attempting to delay the inevitable. Charlie and Aria stepped out of the house, approaching to say their goodbyes. Jenna and Sidney would be leaving Glenwood today, unknowing of when, or if, they would ever return. Over the last few weeks, Jenna opened up to Sidney, telling him they needed this fresh start, a chance to put all the madness of Glenwood behind them. Sidney had been on his best behavior, even when a local man by the name of Brett had been arrested for smacking his family around. In previous conversations, Jenna had brought up the fact that she believed that Sidney had a hero complex, always having to fix everything and help everyone. He had caught on to the fact that Jenna probably knew more than she wanted to admit, especially after the Logan incident, but she kept that to herself, and he appreciated that. It annoyed him when she told him to keep his nose out of the Brett situation, but Sidney listened. They only had a short time left in Glenwood, and he was looking forward to living his life with Jenna and didn't want to complicate it.

Charlie and Sidney gave the typical bro hug, while Jenna and Aria gushed over the adventure that they were taking. One last hug from Tammy for Jenna, before Jenna jumped in the car. Lucia slowly hovered, her face filled with sadness. "Be good," she said, opening her arms to him.

"I promise to be on my best behavior," Sidney said with a chuckle. He wrapped his arms around her and could feel the distance that had grown between them. Jenna was not the only person who voiced her opinion. Lucia had proved many times over that she knew more than she told. She never asked, so Sidney never had to lie. The last thing he wanted to do was hurt the woman who opened up her home, who showed him love, the woman who became a mother to him so many years ago. The distance he felt between them hurt, but he understood. He was not a good guy and did not deserve the love that he had received. But, he knew deep down, he had done right to protect those who would be willing to love someone like him, even if it meant leaving them in the dark, shielding them from his dirty secrets.

Letting go of Lucia, Sidney hopped into the car. The money they saved from the previous summer was safely stashed for their cross-country trip. He backed out of the driveway, and onward they headed, with Glenwood in their rear-view mirror. With the open road before them, many wonderful opportunities awaited them. Sidney remained hopeful that this path they were taking would pave the way to a life that Jenna deserved, even with him.

"It will be different, I promise," Sidney said as they interlocked fingers.

Jenna gave a small nod in the brief eye contact they made.

Sidney knew deep down, Jenna knew what he was promising. He had to change himself, to give her the life she deserved, even if it pained him to make those choices.

Their month of adventure was coming to an end, as they took the exit on the off ramp labeled "Trenmont City." They were both a week away from the beginning of the new school year. Sidney was more excited to get out of the car than he was for school. Jenna had also grown tired of sleeping in it. They were both looking forward to having a nice hot shower that wasn't at a campsite or truck stop. It wasn't that they didn't enjoy themselves, but every person would eventually miss the comforts they had grown accustomed to. They had spent the last month seeing the country, and it was Jenna's idea to sleep in the car so they would not have to spend outrageous amounts of money on hotels every night. If it wasn't for their planning and living minimalistic over the last month, they would have blown through their money rather quickly. They were arriving in Trenmont City with a few hundred dollars in their possession still.

First semester came and went, and both were doing very well in school, so they both began jobs right where they were at. Jenna got a job at the school store, and Sid, who was teased relentlessly over his name when they first arrived, got a job in the kitchen. Just as before, any money they received, they saved. School was uneventful for Jenna and Sid, as they were not big into parting. Between work and school, they spent most of their free time together. They both decided not to head home for breaks, as they were still saving up their money, which was the excuse they gave their families. Video calling was how they communicated for the holidays, as they spent it at their dorm, with what few acquaintances they had made.

Second semester grades, Jenna was struggling. She needed to take a class that summer in order to stay at the same level as her peers, which meant she would need to cut down hours at the store and focus more on her classes. They had already begun to look for an apartment, but Sid pushed her in the direction of focusing on school while he got a second job in the city at a fast-food place. He also picked up a small class that he didn't need in order to stay in his dorm, so Jenna would have one less thing to worry about. He wanted her to focus and achieve what he knew she could.

The third semester ended with both excelling in their classes. Sid continued to work both jobs and juggle school, while Jenna picked up her old job at the store, but with fewer hours. Sid, keeping himself busy, kept his nose out of all the drama that was happening around him. He was too distracted to keep up-to-date, and Jenna knew better than to share certain kinds of information with him. Again, they would not head home for the holidays. This year, their jobs became the excuse for having to stay in the city.

The end of the fourth semester flew up on them more quickly than they had prepared for. Both had put in the effort of finding a place close to the schools. Both were set to graduate with their diplomas, but in order for Sidney to succeed in his career, he would need to further expand his education. They were able to find a one-bedroom apartment, just on the edge of the city, in an apartment building that had openings. It was a tiny space, but was well below the budget they had set. Because they had saved so much money by getting a smaller place, Sid was able to do something he never saw himself doing. He proposed to Jenna and without any hesitation, she said, "Yes!" Things were slowly coming together, but Sid's new internship would rock the boat once more.

A few months passed from college graduation, and Jenna had settled well into her job at one of the local pharmacies. Sid was taking night classes at the college while working his internship during the day. Slowly, their apartment was coming together. Tammy and Lucia had made a surprise visit just the week before and took them both to pick some furniture out. Other than the bed they had purchased, and the odds and ends for the kitchen, they had really nothing in their apartment. They did not want to ask anyone for help and wanted to build it from the ground up together. Two pushy moms changed that, and now they had a complete living room set, as well as a dining room set that would be delivered within four weeks.

Sid hated his internship. He hated the cubicle type job where everyone dressed in stuffy suits and brown-nosed their way to the top. He needed this internship, though, to build relationship and trust, if he ever wanted to venture out on his own. The boss, Anthony Weiner, was a scruffy slob with little tact about him. Sid understood that, as an intern, he would be stuck with grunt work, but Anthony took it to a whole new extreme. One cool October morning, Sid had enough.

"You know what, *Anthony?*" he hissed through closed teeth. "Do it your damn self!" He shoved the pile of papers back at him and turned away before Anthony even had a chance to grab them. With his back turned, Sid could hear the rustling of papers as they tumbled from Anthony's grasp. He walked straight out the door and headed home. In the back of his mind, the thought lingered that he was more than likely going to lose his internship, but it was better than losing what little bit of dignity he had left at that place. Sure enough, by the time he got home, an email awaited him. It was from Anthony, and all it said was:

*"**See me tomorrow.**
8am - my office."*

It was still early in the day, so he changed quickly and headed out to get a drink at the bar down the block. He knew Jenna would be upset, but he hoped she would understand that Sid was not the type to deal with that type of behavior, not anymore. As Sid entered the bar, a big, burly man with a deep Australian accent greeted him. The last time he was here, he learned his name was Miles, and this was his brother's bar. His brother, Thomas, had been in an ATV accident and would have a long road to recovery. Thankfully, Miles could bring his work with him to take care of the bar for Thomas.

After a few drinks, Sid headed home for the inevitable. Facing Jenna's wrath was the only thing Sid actually feared in life. She took it remarkably well, though.

"So, he wants you to meet him in his office?" Jenna held up a glass of wine to Sid.

Sid raised his hands and gave a quick

shake of his head. "No, thank you, and yes. That is all the email said."

"Just don't go breaking any fingers or anything, okay?" Jenna chuckled into her glass of wine.

Sid jumped up from the bar stool and rushed around, scooping her up into a bear hug. Laughs escaped from the two of them as Jenna tried to claw her way out of his grasp without spilling her wine. He would never tire of her laughter. "Your jokes," he said as he set her back onto her feet, "are almost as lame as your taste in alcohol."

Jenna scoffed, "I'm highly sophisticated, compared to your neanderthal ass."

"Oh, I love it when you use big words on me," Sid said as he placed his hand on her lower back. "What else am I?"

She giggled. "A masochist, obviously."

"Mmm... more." Sid nuzzled her neck as she screeched and gave him a nice whack on his shoulder.

"Don't do that!" she squealed.

Taking a step back, he glanced at her with a venomous flare in his eyes. "Are you going to beat me some more?"

Jenna picked up her book and whacked him once more on the shoulder. "Don't get all hot and bothered." She passed him but stopped to lean into his ear. "Wouldn't want to inspire your inner serial killer, now would we?" With a giggle, she scurried her way to the couch.

Sid just shook his head with a chuckle and began to shuffle around the kitchen to make something small to eat. Jenna caught his attention once more.

"Just go in there with your head held high. Apologize and be the bigger man. You may not like him, but you need this internship for your class." Taking a sip of her wine, the two made eye contact. "Everything will work out in the end. I have faith in you, you just need to believe in yourself, too." With that, she went back to her book.

She continued to amaze him every day. She was always optimistic, despite what was happening around them. He strived every day to be the man she deserved, and he could only hope he would make her proud, come tomorrow. Tomorrow certainly was going to be surprising for everyone.

He did just as Jenna told him to. He had his head held high as he entered Anthony's office. The smug bastard was reclined in his chair but hopped up the moment he saw Sid. Anthony came straight for Sid, and he half expected to get punched in the face, but instead, Mr. Weiner held out his hand. Sid was in a state of confusion, but he took his hand as Anthony spoke, "It's Sid, right? So, Sid, you got some spunk, and here, we like that. We prefer people with gumption, which you obviously have. You know how long it has been since an intern has stood up to me? *Me?*" Anthony let out a chuckle as he plopped back down into his chair. His ramblings continued as Sid sat down across from him, mouth hanging open. "So, let me tell you this, Sid. We want to expand on what you do here, okay? We got a nice spot in the corner set up for you.

Let's put that degree of yours to good use. I want to see if you are going to be worth the money, if we were to bring you onto the team."

Sid gave a quick nod.

"We can talk about the books, the investors, the clients, and the contracts that we will have you working on later... over drinks tonight. Sound good?"

Sid just nodded; confusion still pressed into his facial features.

Anthony continued without missing a beat, "Kim will show you to the office, where you can start to look over the contract our current client has us working on, and if you have any questions, we can address them over drinks."

In the blink of an eye, he was out of Anthony's office and in his own, which Kimberly had led him to. There were a couple stacks of papers on the desk and a company laptop with a note telling him the rules of using the laptop. Sid, being the person he was, was skeptical. He had no idea what he just got himself into.

Over drinks, he learned more about the clients and their intentions. Any information he was lacking from his day of scouring through paperwork was answered without fault. He wondered if Anthony was actually a decent person, just a hard ass to his employees. Sid, though, was not a person who let down his guard easily. He would continue to watch his back, because he was in a sea with sharks, and he did not want to get bit. It would take only two months for life to explode.

"I'm their scapegoat!" Sid screamed

into the phone.

"Honey, please, just relax. Come home, and we will talk about this," Jenna begged with him through the phone.

Only silence on the other end of the phone, as Sid thought of what to say next. He was so furious about the whole matter. Turns out, Anthony and his rich buddies had been taking money from clients, money that they shouldn't have taken. Sid noticed some discrepancies and tracked them. He found several offshore accounts that were under his name. The paper trail that had been started was made to look like it was Sid who was stealing the money. Anthony set him up from the very beginning, and he was not going to get away with it.

"Sid?"

Sid huffed. "I'm almost to the office. I'm bringing home whatever papers I have so they don't get rid of them."

"Please come straight home, okay?" Jenna's voice was pleading, and it broke his heart. "Don't do anything rash. Let's talk about it and call the proper people tomorrow morning, okay?"

Sid took in a deep breath as he opened the door to the building. "Okay," and with that, he headed upstairs to gather the papers he needed to hopefully prove his innocence. The last thing he expected was for Anthony Weiner to be in his office at eleven at night. He saw the light illuminating from the office in the corner but shook his head and went straight for the room that they set him up in. He began to pack up what he needed but would come to a halt nearing the end when a voice broke through the loud thumping of his heartbeat.

"Sid! What are you doing here so late, buddy?"

Sid froze in place, anger rising from deep within him. He turned his body slowly, a twisted smile creeping across his face. In the back of his mind, a voice screamed to go home to Jenna. But tonight, he was not going to listen. "Wanted to make sure everything was in order."

"In order for what?" Anthony said, confusion crossing his face.

"The police," Sid replied nonchalantly.

"Police?!" Anthony screamed out.

"You didn't hear?" Sid came out from behind his desk. "I'm funneling money into an offshore account." Sid picked at his fingernails. "Funny thing, though… Some of the money started just a few days before I began interning here." He snapped his eyes back to Anthony, fury burning through them. "Any idea how that could happen?" Sid let out a harsh, disturbing laugh.

Anthony backed away, hands raised defensively. "Now, Sid, it's not what you think."

Sid stalked towards him, like a hunter to his prey. Anthony headed out to a desk and picked up a phone, but Sid appeared by his side quickly and shoved him to the ground, ripping the phone from his grasp. He took the phone and gently placed it back on the receiver. "You want to know what I think?"

Fear could be seen on Anthony's face, while Sid's face twisted into something sinister. His pale blue eyes made him manic looking under the florescent lights. "Sid, I..."

"Shh, it's okay." Sid leaned down to him and brushed Anthony's hair back into place. "I would fear death, too, if I was staring at it right in the face."

CHAPTER SEVENTEEN

When Sid stumbled into his home that night, Jenna was sitting on the couch, still awake. He tossed his box of papers on the counter, and they just locked eyes. He had failed her, but she could never know. The pain that already crossed her face broke his heart.

"I called Tommy's Bar looking for you," Jenna said as she put her head down.

Sid kicked off his shoes and sat down next to her. "And...?"

She looked up at him, her eyes pleading. "You got your papers and came straight home, right?"

Sid nodded slowly.

Sitting up, Jenna placed a kiss on his head, before burying her face into his chest, and he just held her there. Nothing more was said between them. They would fall asleep on the couch together and would only be awoken from Sid's phone ringing the following morning.

When he finally made it into the office, police were all over. Sid carried the box he had originally brought home with him last night. He was approached rather quickly and taken into another room. The camera in the elevator had caught Sid's movement the night before, and they needed Sid to tell his side of the story, explain what he was doing here so late. This would be a game that Sid could play very well, and so the story began.

Yes, Sid came back that night. He explained to the investigator he needed the papers to prove that money was being stolen from a client they assigned him to. Pulling out a few papers from his box, Sid was able to show a money trail that would be an attempt to frame him, but he had also shown that it started before he officially started there. He had already been accepted to do the internship but hadn't had his first day yet, so he had no access to sensitive information at that time. Yes, Sid and Anthony got into a fight. Sid explained to the investigator that when Sid confronted Anthony, Anthony swung at him, so he punched him in the face a few times. He told the investigator that, if Anthony wanted to press charges, he was fine with that, but he was not going to get blamed for funneling money when he did not do it. That is when the investigator thought he would drop a bomb on Sid.

"He's dead."

"Dead?!" Sid hollered.

The gentleman nodded.

Sid's threat to expose Anthony proved to be too much for him to handle. Knowing that he was on a sinking ship, Anthony took his own life, and even left a note admitting to the crimes.

Sid acted surprised, "He admitted it, that he was funneling money?"

"From the account you were working on and over a dozen others. He stapled his note to a stack of accounts that money was being stolen from. Did he seem distressed when you left?"

Sid nodded. "Of course he was distressed. I told him I was going to the police in the morning. I went home with that box so I could bring it to the police department today. I came straight here when I received the phone call, though."

The interview with the investigator was short and sweet. Whispers of Anthony's suicide floated throughout the office. If only they knew, he didn't take his life willingly.

"Stand up like a man!" Sid shouted through gritted teeth.

"I wrote the note admitting I did it! What more do you want?!" Anthony shrieked.

"People like you never learn." Sid placed his knife under Anthony's throat once more. "Stand... up..."

Anthony did as he was told and stood on the chair in front of his desk. His body was shaking as he sobbed.

Sid ran the knife down Anthony's arm slowly, without touching his skin, just enough to cause Anthony's hairs to rise. "Now put your beautiful necklace on..." Sid's voice was harsh, his face twisted with a pleasureful smile.

Tears streamed down Anthony's face once more as his sobs grew. "Please," he begged.

"NOW!" screamed Sid, spittle flying from his lips.

Anthony inserted his head into his "necklace" while continuing to plead with Sid. Without a second thought, Sid kicked the chair out from under him and walked right out of the office without looking back.

Jenna only asked once about Anthony Weiner, and Sid would tell her that his death was being ruled a suicide. She would never bring it up again.

A few months passed, and Sid came home from the office, where he was now employed because of his diligence, and came to find someone in their apartment with Jenna. Since moving into the building, Sid and Jenna had kept to themselves. Between working long hours and college courses, they really didn't have much time.

"Sid!" Jenna shrilled, rushing over to him. "This is Scarlett, they just moved in upstairs."

The young girl waved at him shyly.

Sid smiled softly. "Nice to meet you, Scarlett."

"Sorry for the intrusion," Scarlett said.

Jenna interjected, "No intrusion at all!" Jenna turned back to Sid. "I volunteered you to help her husband." Jenna batted her eyes and gave him an innocent smile.

Sid's eyebrows raised as he let out a chuckle. "Volunteered? For what?"

"You don't have to if you don't want to." Scarlett stood, her hands raised. Sid was taken aback for a moment, because from her seated position, he did not see it. Now that she was standing, her swollen belly was extremely visible.

"Their movers canceled last minute. That truck outside has their stuff in it, and obviously, she can't really carry too much." Jenna looped her arm around his. "So, what do…"

"It's fine." Sid smiled down at Jenna.

"Just let me get changed, and I will give..." Sid looked up to Scarlett.

"Oh, Mason."

"Mason, a hand," Sid continued.

"It doesn't have to be all today." Scarlett shifted her feet, visibly uncomfortable. "We have the truck until Sunday."

"Well, let me know where I can find Mason, and we will get done what we can." He placed a kiss on top of Jenna's head. "I just got to change first and take out Mrs. Garcia's trash. It is Wednesday, after all."

"Thank you," Scarlett said with a smile. "We are one floor up, second door to the left of the elevator. Mason should be there, or will be there, as he carries up boxes."

Sid got changed quickly and headed out the door to meet up with Mason. Just as Sid went to step off the elevator, he came face to face with a younger man, roughly the same age as the woman in his apartment. "Are you Mason?"

The man gave a small smile; he looked exhausted. "Sid, I'm guessing?"

Sid gave a nod and stepped back into the elevator. "We can get as much done as you are able to and can work on more tomorrow and Sunday, as those are my days off."

"I really appreciate it." Mason ran his lengthy fingers through his hair. "I don't want to steal your weekend from you, though."

Sid chuckled, leaning onto the railing of the elevator. "We don't do much, anyways.

We are homebodies. Plus, I do whatever the lady says."

Mason gave a heartfelt laugh. "I feel you. The things we do for our women, huh?"

With that, the elevator door opened, and they stepped off and headed towards the exit. "Hold up a moment," Sid said as he turned towards the back of the building. "I have to pick up some trash from an apartment down here."

Mason followed Sid as they headed towards the rear of the apartment complex. "I help Mrs. Garcia down here with her trash every week and little things when she asks. She is a very stubborn..." Rounding the corner, Sid stopped dead in his tracks. Something wasn't right.

"You okay?" Mason said, cautiously.

Sid rushed up to her apartment door, which was just barely open. "Maria?!" he shouted, slowly pushing open the door. He waited for a response before pushing the door open all the way. "Do me a favor?" he said to Mason.

"Yeah?" Mason said as he approached behind him.

"Take the left of the apartment? Maria never leaves her door unlocked, let alone open." Sid cautiously moved deeper into the apartment.

Heading farther into the apartment, they reached the hallway that split the apartment in half. Mason headed left down the hallway, and Sid to the right. He only made it partway into her bedroom when he heard Mason call out, "Sid! In here! Call 911!"

Sid took off down the hallway towards the living room, fumbling to get his phone out of his pocket. Finally reaching Mason, Sid dialed and watched in fear as Mason did CPR on the elderly woman. As he talked with the operator, his eyes wandered around the apartment and noticed that it was completely trashed. Drawers had been pulled out, couch cushions flung around the room, and papers scattered all over the floor. As he continued to talk to the operator, he headed back to the front door and, sure enough, there were scuff and scrape marks, as if someone had forced themselves inside. His heart raced as he realized that someone may have hurt Mrs. Garcia. After hanging up with the operator, he searched the apartment, top to bottom, looking for anyone who didn't belong but found no one.

The rest of the night was pure agony. When first responders arrived, they tried everything they could, but they could not bring her back. Mason and Sid both had to speak to police about what they had seen and explain why they were in her apartment to begin with. Sid was absolutely furious, demanding that they find whoever did this and to stop standing around asking questions. Jenna did her best to calm him, but Jenna herself was very distraught. She had grown attached to Mrs. Garcia, due to the fact that they had dinner together at least once a week, if not more, on nights that Sid had to work late. Mason was having a hard time wrapping his head around everything that had just happened. He voiced his concerns to Jenna and Sid. Jenna tried to lessen the strain, explaining that this was a good neighborhood and a very safe building, because of the security involved with getting into the building. You needed a key or code to access the building. Nothing ever happened around this area, which was the same reason they chose it as well. It just seemed unreal that someone could break into the building and then turn around and break into an apartment. Mason raised the idea that maybe they already had access to the building, which would put Sid on the task of searching the building, high and low, for any signs of the robber. It would take him weeks, but he finally found him.

Almost two months would go by before they would have any answers surrounding Maria's death. Turns out that no one physically harmed her. The only conclusion the medical examiner could come up with was that Maria was either not home at the time of the intrusion or didn't hear the person enter. Maria had died of a heart attack. Her heart was already weak, and whatever had happened in the apartment sent a chain of events in motion that would ultimately leave her dead. It relieved Jenna and Sid to know that she wasn't harmed physically, but there were still no suspects for the break in and theft. There had been no fingerprints left at the scene, and they combed the place for DNA. The only DNA they found was from those who had been in the house with Mrs. Garcia on other days. Jenna had been in her apartment enough to know quite a bit of what was missing. To help the police, Jenna and Sid kept their eyes peeled for any of the items on sites online. There was nothing. Sid was determined to bring whoever had committed this act to justice and even went as far as visiting local pawn shops and leaving his information. He hoped that someday, the person would slip up, and five months after the break in, he finally did.

"You have a name and address?" Sid said, leaning over his desk with a pen and paper.

"You're going to give this information to the police, correct?" the gentleman said on the other end of the phone.

"Of course. They will more than likely be reaching out to you to confirm this, so make sure you answer."

The man gave him the information that he had acquired from the customer, and Mason was correct in his assumption. The person who went to pawn off some of Mrs. Garcia's jewelry lived in the apartment building, just a few floors below Sid and Jenna.

As he agreed, he called the police right after and gave the information he had, including the location of the pawnshop. He was trying to leave it in the hands of the proper people, like Jenna had asked. As he sat at this desk, though, it was slowly away at eating him on the inside. Would the cops go and arrest him, or would he get away with it? He couldn't continue to sit here and wait. When he finally arrived at the apartment complex, there was not a single police car, so he took it upon himself to do a little investigating. Hopping off the elevator on the fifth floor, Sid pulled out the little paper where he had written the information:

Liam Hall
Apt: 504

He stood directly in front of the apartment door. The little voice inside his head screamed to go to his own apartment, to stay out of it, but a louder voice screamed back. Sid knocked on the door lightly, taking long, deep breaths, in an attempt to stay calm. He could feel his heart begin to race, and his palms became sweaty. He ran his knuckles over his pocketknife that was clipped to his belt, making sure he had it on him, in case he needed it. Patience was not something he was good at, and when he just about lost it, he heard shuffling behind the door. A big, muscular looking man opened the door and greeted Sid with a smile that twisted his stomach.

"Can I help you?" Liam said with a smile.

Sid forced a smile across his lips. "Hi, yes. I am sorry to disturb you. I was wondering if you had any flour? I am trying to surprise my girl with dinner, and I can't find anything in her apartment."

The man let out a chuckle and opened his door. "Sure, man. Come on in, and I

191

will get you a bowl."

Sid closed the door behind him and walked slowly into Liam's apartment as he shuffled around the get the flour. Sid's eyes scanned all around, analyzing every aspect of the apartment. "How long have you lived here?" Sid said, picking up a picture frame to get a better look.

"I've been here for almost four years." Liam looked over towards Sid. "My sister, she lives a few hours away."

Sid made eye contact as he set the frame back down. "Four years, huh? Exciting stuff normally happen here?"

Liam turned his back to Sid, pouring the flour into a plastic bowl. "Exciting?"

Sid leaned against the island in the center of the kitchen. "You didn't hear about the break in downstairs?"

Liam lost his grip on the bag of flour, and it fell with a thud to the counter. "Ugh, no... I had not heard about it. I keep to myself mostly."

Sid picked at a crumb on the counter before him. "Yeah, stole stuff from an old lady. Left her to die on the floor."

Sid and Liam made eye contact. He could see it in Liam's eyes, the guilt building up. "Oh..."

Sid flicked the crumb in Liam's direction. "So, where's her stuff, *Liam?*" His name was like venom on his tongue.

Liam turned away quickly and placed the top on the bowl of flour. Sid watched as his shoulders rapidly rose and fell with each breath. Then, his shoulders hunched over, defeat written in his posture. "She wasn't supposed to be there."

"So, you left her there to die on the cold floor? All alone?" Sid watched for movement, but he just stood with his back towards him, his head hanging still.

Liam sighed, "I panicked and just ran with what I had in my bag." Liam turned around slowly, head still facing downward. "I know I can never make up for what I did. My sister needs money. I can't let her go without."

Sid looked back at the stand that held the picture of Liam and his sister, willing himself to leave the apartment. The police, though, they hadn't even been here, yet. They knew who they were after, the guilty party, and they sat on their asses, like always. Sid whipped his head back around, his piercing blue eyes boring into Liam. "Where is her stuff?"

"On the roof." Liam still would not make eye contact.

The big, muscular man who had answered the door was no longer standing before Sid. It was a weak, pathetic piece of trash, but his sister, he could sympathize with. If he just got Maria's stuff, he would be willing to end it there.

"You give me her stuff, and I won't tell the police. Find a different way to help your sister. Sound fair?" Sid stood tall, stuffing his hands into his pockets.

Liam's attitude completely changed. He perked right up with a smile and looked directly at Sid. "Follow me, and you can have it." Liam walked right past Sid and headed out of the apartment towards the stairs.

Sid analyzed his every movement as

they reached the roof. His attitude flipped too quickly. Something just didn't seem right.

Once they reached the roof, Sid struck up a conversation. "So, what does your sister need?"

"What?" Liam turned back towards him, confusion crossing his face.

"Your sister? What does she need?" Sid reiterated.

"Oh, um... like girl stuff." Liam fumbled with the gate that blocked in the water tower.

"And she lives where? Maybe I can help her?" Sid stared at Liam, watching his body expressions.

"Oh, like a block or two away."

Liam just lost the sympathy card. Everything that came out of his mouth was a lie, a way to twist his way out of the wrong he had done. He had caused a death this time. What would happen the next time? "Where is her stuff?"

"In the water tank," Liam said plainly.

"In the tank?" Sid was shocked that someone would think of that as a stashing spot.

"Yeah. I threw it in a bag and sealed it up nice and tight before throwing it in there. Nobody ever checks the water tanks. I've been stashing stuff in them for years." Liam headed up the ladder as Sid watched from below. As Liam reached the hatch, he fumbled around to get inside. Slowly, Sid crept up the ladder below him, quietly, as to not make a sound. Liam reached inside to grab the bag but was struggling to reach it. Liam climbed up to the very top of the ladder and was hanging inside the tank. It was just too easy. With one quick, light push, Liam fell with a splash into the tank. Without touching the hatch, he nudged it closed and headed down the ladder. Sid could hear his scream echoing, which became fainter with each step he took. The first thing to cross his mind when he reached the door to the building was he could really use a beer.

CHAPTER EIGHTEEN

"Do you believe there was any speculation as to your involvement in Liam's death?" Jack said.

Sid's head shook. "No. Turns out that my 'tip' about him being involved in Maria's death was misplaced." Sid scoffed. "Doesn't surprise me one bit."

"And the official report that was released, did you find out what it said?"

"Of course. I needed to make sure no fingers pointed back to me." Sid paused, his eyes lowering to his fingers as he picked at his cuticle.

"And?" Jack said, leaning forward.

"It was labeled as an accident, especially because he was found with stolen property." Sid looked up at Jack, giving a shrug. "No skin off my back."

"What has you upset about that situation, though? When you discuss it, it seems to have a negative reaction."

Sid stared at Jack. He took a deep breath before responding, "Jenna said that is when I started to slip."

"What do you mean by 'started to slip?'" Jack asked quizzically.

"We were building a life together. We had steady jobs, a nice place to live, and we had made our first friends since high school. Over the next eight months, though, four people would die."

Jack leaned back in his chair. "Including Andy."

Sid looked down at his fingers once more. "Andy..."

⇥ ⇥⇥ ⇥ ⇥⇥ ⇥⇥

Sid answered his phone, placing it to his ear as he headed down the sidewalk. "Did you forget something today?"

"No, Sid. It's Andy." Jenna's voice was hushed. He could hear her rustling around.

"Andy?" He hadn't seen Andy since junior year, before he hopped town. He had attempted to get a hold of him for a few months after he left, but had no luck. Eventually, his voicemail box filled up, and then, shortly after, his phone was disconnected. He had no idea where he was, so he stopped looking. Charlie gave up looking for him shortly after, as well. It wasn't that they didn't care about their friend, but they all had lives and school, which took up a lot of time. Sid still thought of him from time to time, but there had been no trace of him anywhere.

"He's here," Jenna said as she interrupted his thoughts.

Sid stopped dead in the middle of the sidewalk. "Here? As in, the apartment?"

"Yes, he's in the living room right now," Jenna said, her voice lowering even more. "I couldn't turn him away, he's-"

"He's what? Jenna?" Sid walked down the sidewalk once more, his pace quicker than before. He was still three blocks from the apartment complex.

"Sorry, I thought I heard someone coming up the hallway." Jenna sighed heavily. "He looks horrible, Sid. He needs help. I couldn't..."

"It's okay, Jenna. I will be there in ten minutes." Sid stopped for the light in front of him. "Make him something to eat, if he wants. Just stall him until I get there."

Hanging up, Sid stood waiting for the sign across the street to light up to give him the right-away to walk. He absolutely hated trying to cross certain cross walks. The pedestrian lights in Trenmont City did not seem to care if you pressed the button or not. They seemed to have their own mind. They took forever and only gave pedestrians all of two seconds to cross. It was like signing a death warrant if you couldn't cross in time. After what seemed like an eternity, the light gave Sid the right-away, and he picked up his pace to a jog, trying to get to the apartment to see Andy. If Jenna thought he needed help, he would take her at her word, and they would do whatever they could to help their old friend.

Finally reaching his building, he rushed inside and up the stairs as quickly as he could. Reaching for his door, he stopped short when it swung open in front of him. He came face to face with someone he could barely recognize. Dirt and grime smeared the man's skin and clothes, his hair was long and matted in some spots. A smell wafted in the surrounding air. It smelled like a mix of an ashtray, cheap booze, and stale urine. The eyes were the only thing he recognized from his old friend, but the pain that was mixed into them made Sid ache to his bones. The figure attempted to pass Sid, but Sid placed an arm between the exit and the man. The man's eyes shot up at Sid and looked as if he had just come between a starving dog and a scrap of meat. "Andy?" Sid said, his voice soft.

"Please, just stay." Jenna appeared behind Andy, she looked disheveled herself. What had happened between them?

"No," Andy's head shook rapidly. "I shouldn't have come." Andy shoved Sid's arm out of the way and headed down the hallway.

"Let us help!" Sid called after him, as he followed him.

"Help?" Andy turned back towards Sid with a chuckle. He took a rather large step towards Sid. "You want to help? I need money."

Sid took a step back. He wanted to keep

his distance between himself and Andy. The man in front of him was not the same person from high school. A lot must have happened to Andy for him to get to this place in his life. Sid did not want to pity him, but that was the strong feeling that was overwhelming him. "What is the money for, Andy?"

"Does it matter?" Andy snapped at him.

"How about we start with dinner?" Sid said, holding his arm out in an attempt to direct Andy back to the apartment. "Let's all get something to eat, talk a bit, and see what else we can do to help." Andy was like a wild animal with his movements as he looked around the hallway, at Jenna who was standing in the doorway, tearful, and at Sid who kept a distance, uneasy, knowing that Andy's behavior would be highly unpredictable. It was as if he was analyzing them, making sure they were not a threat to him.

With a little hesitation shown in his movements, Andy headed back into the apartment, with Sid on his heels. With the door closed behind Andy, he seemed like a deer in an unfamiliar place, eyes darting around with every new sound, assessing every movement. He refused to sit down, and like a caged animal, paced back and forth in front of the door. But even with the actions he was portraying, Sid still wanted to help him.

>+> >+> >+> >+> >+>

"So, he stayed for dinner. Once the food was out and placed on the table, that is when he sat down. He would only sit in the seat closest to the door, though. I made small talk, to try to get him to open up. I had no idea what to say after all those years." Sid hung his head. "We tried so hard to get him to stay, but he refused. He kept insisting he needed money."

Jack shifted in his seat. "Did you end up giving him any money?"

Sid shook his head. "We aren't ones to carry cash. He got furious and ran off just as my phone rang, when we told him we weren't going to give him any money. I didn't even see Jenna running after him, I was so distracted."

"Let's start with who was on the phone, okay?" Jack said, leaning forward.

Sid leaned back into his seat. "It was Charlie. He wanted to know if I had seen Andy. Turns out, Andy owes a lot of money to a dealer here in Trenmont City. Charlie figured there would be a chance he would show up at our place."

"So, that would explain Andy's behavior, wouldn't you say?"

Sid nodded. "After the phone call, I put two and two together. He needed money to get his next hit." Sid's head shook. "I realized, while on the phone with Charlie, that Jenna was gone. I told him she probably went after Andy. Charlie was right around the corner, as he had been looking for Andy, so he headed towards the apartment building."

Jack made a few notations on his paper before speaking. "When Charlie arrived, was Andy there?"

Sid shook his head, "No." Sid's fists balled together on the table. He stared down at his hands, the whites of his knuckles very apparent.

"Sid, take a deep breath. We get through this day, and I won't push anymore." Jack sat on the edge of his seat.

Taking a long, deep breath, Sid laid his hands flat on the table between them. "When Charlie arrived, Andy was gone. Jenna was at the bottom of the steps, bleeding, and he was gone." Sid looked straight at Jack, his face blank as he continued, "She said she fell trying to stop him. Jenna supposedly grabbed him, and he hollered at her. Scarlett witnessed it and backed up her story."

Jack finally relaxed back into his chair. "Very good, Sid. Now, what did he yell at her about?"

"Andy asked her how she could be with a guy like me, someone who never took responsibility when I did wrong." Anger was building in Sid once more.

"What was he referring to?" Jack asked.

"The people I killed, the ones I got away with," Sid said nonchalantly.

"When did you find out he knew about the deaths?"

"He never knew, he just had a feeling I was involved. He admitted to his speculations the day I ripped him from the inside out after the funeral. He should have never hurt her." Sid stood from his chair, his palms flat on the table in front of them, his piercing blue eyes glaring at Jack. "He hurt her, not once, but twice! He deserved so much more than what I gave him. He touched what was mine! I may be a bad guy, but I would never hurt an innocent! Never!"

>+->+>->+->+>->+->+>->+

"Jenna!" shouted Charlie. His voiced echoed up the stairwell as Sid rushed down the steps, almost falling over himself. When he finally reached the bottom steps, he could see Scarlett hovered over his blonde-haired angel. Charlie made eye contact, and he could see the concern in his eyes.

"Where's Andy?" Sid said, as he placed a hand on Charlie's shoulder. When he looked down at Jenna, this time from her side, he could see the blood on her blouse. Sid quickly dropped to her side. "What happened?"

"I fell, I'm fine!" Jenna attempted to stand, putting her hands into the air.

"Pressure!" Scarlett yelled at her. "Bloody noses can get the best of you. Just don't tip your head back. Lean forward and keep pressure." Scarlett turned her attention to Sid as she helped Jenna sit back down. "She will be fine, but your friend is gone."

"He must have run the opposite way." Charlie raked his hand through his hair.

Sid stood, coming eye level with Charlie. "What is this?" Sid said with a chuckle, flipping a piece of Charlie's long hair from in front of his face.

"Aria loves it," Charlie said with a smirk.

"Can we go upstairs, please?" Jenna said, pleading. "I'd rather not sit all night on the stairs."

Sid bent down and scooped up Jenna. Scarlett reminded them to monitor Jenna before she headed out the door to her floor, while the others headed up to Sid and Jenna's apartment. When they finally reached their floor, Charlie spoke, all breathy from the workout that was the stairs, "Do you have an elevator?"

"You can take the risk, but the damn thing breaks at least twice a week," Sid said with a chuckle. "Takes the damn fire department between two and three hours each time to get us out."

They headed into the apartment, and Sid sat Jenna down. Even with the excitement that was Andy, it turned out to be a nice evening. Charlie and Sid caught up while Jenna iced her face. Thirty minutes passed before Aria showed up, and Sid had to save her because she got lost in the building.

Sid and Charlie discussed what had been going on with Andy. Sid had been kept out of the loop because he hadn't yet gone home for any of the holidays since moving to Trenmont City. Lucia said she missed Sid, but when Charlie would bring them up, she would brush Charlie off, stating she understood they were busy. Sid asked how she was doing, and Aria told him that Lucia was hiding something. Lucia was never a person to open up about her problems, so he made a note that he needed to call home to check on her. And, if she didn't want to talk, he would head back to Glenwood to find out what was going on. No matter what had happened, Sid still looked to Lucia as his mother, even if he didn't call her that.

It was close to midnight when Charlie's phone rang. They hadn't even realized how late it was, with all the talking and catching up. Charlie's face went pale, though, as he listened to the person on the other end of the phone. Concern built up as Charlie stepped into the back hallway, and Aria admitted she was just as lost as Sid and Jenna were. When Charlie finally returned, Aria was the first to speak.

"Charlie? What's wrong?"

"Andy, he ugh..." Charlie dropped onto the couch next to Aria. He just sat there, his head in his hands, for just a few moments, before quiet sobbing overtook his body. Aria wrapped her arms around him as he spoke into his hands, "Andy stole a car and was trying to get out of Trenmont City. He flipped the car just outside of the city limits." Charlie looked up at Aria, tears running down his cheeks. "They don't know if he is going to make it."

CHAPTER NINETEEN

Jenna just wasn't the same after Andy's visit and the accident. They visited his bedside a few times while he was in the medically induced coma, but it proved to be too much for her. It wasn't that she was overly emotional, she just seemed uneasy being there. When Sid tried to question it, she brushed it off, saying that the hospital made her uncomfortable. He had never heard her mention that before, but he didn't want to bother her with it.

Andy's parents flew in the day after the accident and stayed for as long as they could by his bedside. His mother stayed the entire time, while his father had to return to Glenwood to take care of their store. Sid told Mike that he would continue to check on Wanda and make sure she was taken care of. He brought her items whenever she asked for them, and he stayed by the bedside for her so she could shower occasionally and leave the room. Even when the doctors said Andy was out of the woods, she still was afraid to leave his bedside. Sid could see it plastered against her pale skin. Charlie and Aria stayed for almost a week after the accident. Sid opened up his home to them so they would have somewhere comfortable to stay. Hotels in the city were overpriced, and it was bad enough they flew here, which was a nice chunk of money as well. Charlie and Aria couldn't stay over a week because they each had their own business to get back to. Aria had opened a bakery in Glenwood, and Charlie operated Hudson's old business. Together, they were expanding Hudson's old business and had almost erased the stain his father had left.

After a few weeks, Andy woke up, and he was able to breathe on his own. The surgeries had been successful, but he had a long road to recovery. He would have to learn to walk again, but he was determined to get his life back on track. Jenna paid him a visit after he woke up, but Sid felt that she really didn't want to be there, so he never pushed her to go see him again. Sid continued to offer his support and help if they needed it. Wanda wanted Andy to come back home to Glenwood, but he refused. He was still in no condition to travel too far, and he wanted to continue treatment with the people who had saved his life. Wanda would continue to stay for a little while longer, but Mike would eventually ask her to come home. Wanda left Trenmont City, knowing he had a friend here to help, and that he was in excellent hands with the medical staff around him.

Sid had made plans to head to Glenwood. With his visit from Charlie and Aria, he knew he needed to head home to see Lucia, especially if she was hiding something. No matter what had happened between them, he needed to make sure she was okay. The weekend he was meant to fly to Glenwood, he came home to find cops all around and inside his building. Any plans he had made would now be postponed.

At first, no one would allow Sid into the apartment building. It took speaking to four different officers before they allowed him to enter the building, and even then, they escorted him to his apartment and asked not to leave for a while. Closing the door behind him, Jenna held out a beer, her eyebrows raised. "Hey, honey. How was your day?"

Sid took the beer from her and motioned towards the door. "What the hell? Did someone else in the building die?"

Jenna was already walking away and heading over to the window they converted into a reading nook. "I've been sitting here since I first heard the commotion. They have brought out boxes of stuff, including computers and papers." She took a sip of her wine before continuing, "Haven't seen anyone brought out yet, but they could have them already at the station."

"You've been here, how long?" Sid said as he popped the cap off his beer.

"Um, like..." Jenna ran her finger along the edge of her wineglass, "Three hours."

"Three hours?!"

Jenna shrugged with a laugh. "I'm nosy, you already know that." Jenna jumped up off the nook and screamed, "Oh my god! I know him!"

Sid came up behind her and peeked out towards the sidewalk. He could see a heavyset, brown-haired male being placed in the back of the police cruiser. "You know him?"

Jenna nodded into her wineglass. "He comes into the pharmacy a lot."

"For what?"

She spun around, giving him a whack. "I can't tell you that, and you know it!"

Sid gave a shrug. "Who am I going to tell?"

Jenna glared down her nose at him.

Sid raised his arms defensively with a laugh. "Got it. Not my business."

Jenna walked past him, heading back into the kitchen. "Just like his crimes are not your business," Jenna mumbled.

"What was that?" Sid said, following close behind. He had heard her, but he wanted to see if she would repeat herself. Normally she wouldn't, just like today.

Jenna turned around with a smile plastered on her face. "I saw Scarlett and Mason today. Verity is getting so big." Just as fast as her smile came, it had disappeared. A family, it was all she ever wanted. It hurt him to know that having children of their own might not be possible. They had contemplated fertility treatments, but they were just so expensive. They decided they would get married first, but Jenna had a novel listing everything she wanted. So, they were saving up for her dream wedding. He wanted her to have everything she wanted, except kids. It wasn't that he didn't want to have kids with her, he just didn't see himself as father material. He wouldn't even know how to be a father. He had killed the only father figure he had in his life for being a horrible person.

Sid changed the subject, hoping to bolster her spirits once more. "That promotion was just posted. I am going to interview for it next week."

"Really?!" Jenna screeched as she jumped up and down, ending with a jump that wrapped her arms around him. "I know you've got this promotion in the bag!"

Sid gave her a kiss before insisting that they sit down to eat dinner, as it was getting late. There, though, nagging in the back of his mind, was the image of the man in handcuffs. What had he done that warranted that many officers? It would be almost a week before he would see the man's face again. This time, it wasn't in person, but on the cover of the newspaper. Sid sat at his cubicle in the office, eating his lunch, when he did a double take. He flipped through the paper he had picked up from the break table. He wasn't normally a person to read the paper, but for whatever reason, Sid picked it up to read today. The paper had a huge picture of the man's face and said:

Trenmont City man found in possession of child pornography
William Hendrix, age 37, of Trenmont City, was charged Tuesday by federal officials with receipt, distribution, and possession of child pornography. The charges carry a minimum sentence of ten years and a maximum sentence of forty years in prison, and a fine of up to $250,000.

Assistant U.S. Attorney Melissa Kennedy is handling the case. She said they had received an anonymous tip stating Hendrix was selling images and videos. An undercover, while connected to a peer-to-peer network, was able to get in contact with Hendrix, who distributed images to him, using an encrypted thumb drive. He was arrested last Tuesday on charges of possessing, reproducing, and distributing child pornography.

A federal search warrant was executed at Hendrix's residence. Officers seized digital devices that included four portable hard drives, three thumb drives, a laptop, and a desktop computer. A review determined the devices contained approximately 1,200 images of child pornography and about eight videos of child pornography.

Hendrix appeared in federal court Wednesday afternoon. He was released on electronic home monitoring.

Sid stared at the image as he ate his lunch, the entire time his mind churning. How could someone do something like this? The fact that they allowed him to go home, when there are children in the building, infuriated Sid. They had only charged him with having the images and videos, but had he physically hurt a child? His mind wandered to Mason and Scarlett, the friends they had made, the friends who lived in the same building as this monster. Verity was just a little girl, but could he have set his sights on her? His stomach churned, the rumbling sounding from deep below, becoming increasingly louder, as the stomach acid mixed with his lunch and began to rise. A feeling he had never felt before was overcoming him. He sat, palms flat on his desk, taking deep breaths, when he heard a voice from behind him.

"You okay?"

Sid turned to see Lucas standing in the opening of his cubicle. Most people left Sid alone, as he wasn't a big talker. Lucas had never spoken to Sid before, so it seemed a little strange, but it was a nice comfort to have a distracted mind at that moment. "Upset stomach."

"Here," Lucas said as he reached into his pocket and pulled out a small plastic case. He popped it open to reveal antacids. "My wife packed burritos today, so I had to come prepared." He chuckled as he dumped the medicine into Sid's hand.

"Thank you," Sid said with a nod.

Lucas leaned into Sid's cubicle, looking

over his shoulder. "You reading up on that creep?" he said as he thrusted his head forward, directing to the paper on the table.

Sid raked his hand through his hair. "That creep lives in my building." He sighed before continuing, "I have friends in the building with a little girl, and I just can't even imagine someone hurting her."

"That right there is the type of man that doesn't deserve prison." Lucas shrugged, holding his hands up defensively. "My opinion, but what makes them stop at pictures and videos?"

Sid nodded slowly, his eyes burning into the picture of William Hendrix. Lucas was right. He didn't deserve prison. He deserved death. It would be almost three weeks before Sid would find his opportunity.

Jenna busted through the apartment door, flustered, muttering to herself, "Asshole," being the only part of the sentence that Sid could make out.

Sid sat at the table, shuffling through stacks of paperwork he had to bring home, because of a client changing his mind for the hundredth time in less than a week. "You know, just because I didn't have a chance to make dinner, doesn't give you the right to call me names."

Jenna jumped, startled that he was in the apartment. Her eyes went wide as they adjusted to the sight of what had taken over their dining room table. "What the... I'm not even going to ask. I just, ugh!" Jenna chucked her jacket at the bar stool.

Sid left the table, approaching Jenna from the side. "What happened?"

"What happened?" She scoffed. "I'm a nice person, who thought I was doing someone a favor, but no! He wants to be an asshole. I didn't have to deliver his medication! It is not my fault he is on house arrest! Maybe if he didn't go around sexualizing children, he could pick up his own medication!" Jenna began waving her hands around as she paced back and forth in front of the kitchen island while speaking, "'Where's my metformin?' 'Can't you guys get anything right?' Can you not want to fuck children? That would be even better! Then, you could get your own shit!"

Sid, who had approached to comfort Jenna, now stood wide eyed and speechless as her rant continued.

"Like, is it really that big of a deal that the look of the pills changed? Weren't you taught to read, or is that another skill, like human compassion, that you lack?" Jenna turned to Sid, grabbing him by his upper arms. "Like I have any control over the SHAPE OF THE PILLS!" She threw her hands in the air and began her pacing once more. "Like, Jesus Christ! At least I brought you your medication so you wouldn't DIE!" With one last huff, Jenna threw herself onto the couch.

Sid sat on the arm of the couch, leaning over towards her. "Feel better?"

"Yes," she said, muffled by the couch, as she was face down. Swinging herself around, she sat up and grabbed Sid's hand, which was held out for her. "People can just be so rude."

Sliding down onto the couch, he wrapped his arms around her. "I know. That is why I stick with you. You only tell me off when you think I need it." Sid let out a grunt as Jenna hit him in the stomach. "Okay, okay," he chuckled. "When I know I need it. The little people are so violent." She glared up at him, and he smiled down at her.

"What I just told you needs to stay between us, though. I could get in a lot of trouble at work."

"Who am I going to tell?" Sid pointed to the table. "I could tell the stack of papers."

Jenna hit him again, a little harder on the arm. "Ass."

"Yes." He placed a light kiss atop her head. "I do have a nice ass, but yours is better." Before Jenna could swing at him, he jumped up from the couch. "I'm going to order some takeout because I got work to get done, and I will swap over the laundry after I order it."

"Thai sounds really good!" Jenna said, bouncing on the couch.

"Thai it is." Sid picked up his wallet and phone and headed towards the door. Opening it, he turned back to Jenna, who was sliding out of her work sneakers. "I will make sure to get you whatever you want. Wouldn't want you to chew my head off. Quite feisty today, I see." Jenna picked up a pillow off the couch and threw it at the door, but Sid shut it with a laugh before it could reach him.

Heading down the stairs, Sid multi-tasked and ordered Thai food from the web page for delivery. The last thing he expected when he reached the basement was to come face to face with William Hendrix. Shoving his phone into his pocket, he adverted his gaze and headed over to the washers that held their clothes. He needed to keep his mind occupied, for the sake of Jenna, but a hushed voice would pull him over to that despicable piece of shit.

"Um, I'm sorry to bother you, but do you possibly have two quarters? I just need to finish drying."

Sid took a slow, deep breath but kept his back to William. "Mrs. Abbott upstairs can reload your card in the office. Just have to call her, so she can meet you at the office."

William cleared his throat. "I don't have any money on me at the moment." Silence passed between the two men, and Sid contemplated with himself if he wanted to help at all. He was absolutely repulsed by his behavior, thinking what he did was right, but he was also appalled by the way he treated Jenna. William pulled him from his thoughts. "I know you know who I am. My face is plastered everywhere. I just need fifty cents to get my clothes dried, and then I will get out of your hair."

Sid whipped around furiously and headed straight for William. With his hand in his pocket, he ran his fingers across the blade he carried. When he reached him, he stopped within a few inches of his face and glared down his nose at him. Pulling his hand out of his pocket, he slapped his hand down on top of the folding table to the side of them, revealing two quarters. Taking another deep breath, Sid turned and headed back to his washer.

"Thank you," William said with a weak voice. He slid the quarters into the machine and started the dryer.

"Hey, William?" Sid said, spinning towards him once more.

"Yes?" William said, pivoting towards Sid.

"Next time you want to be rude to my fiancé, don't. She has more compassion in her one little finger than you would ever have in your entire body." Sid cocked his head to the side as a flustered William nodded, wide eyed.

William quickly headed out of the laundry room and up the stairs, while Sid stood there for a moment, proud that he hadn't hit him, or done something worse. His eyes, at that moment, caught something on the other table. A small set of keys sat where William had been standing. Sid stood there for only a minute, debating with himself, but ultimately swiped the keys. The keys may prove useful, if he needed to take care of any business. Sid continued with his laundry, when a frazzled William came into the laundry room once more. He could hear the footsteps behind him, but Sid did not turn around.

"Um, I'm sorry but ugh, have you seen any keys?"

"I have not."

Sid could hear William shuffling around a bit before leaving the laundry room once more. He turned around and looked at the time on William's dryer. If he was going to do this today, he would need to plan it right. Forty minutes on the timer. Forty minutes to figure out how to rid that man, if that is what you could call him, from this world. The first thing that popped into his head was the medication incident from earlier. As he headed up the stairs back to his apartment, he looked up "metformin" to see what exactly it was, and the website said:

Metformin is used with a proper diet and exercise program, and possibly with other medications, to control high blood sugar in people with type two diabetes.

So, he suffered from diabetes and, from the looks of him, there had to be more to the picture. Getting into his apartment would allow for Sid to see exactly what he was working with. He would have a few minutes before Mrs. Abbott would respond to allow William back into his apartment. It was just enough time for Sid to slip in and out of his apartment. While inside, he shuffled around quietly, noticing the smell and the utter disarray that the apartment was in. William was not a person to take care of himself. Continuing to move around the apartment, Sid noticed the number of medications that were sitting out on the counter. Without touching anything, Sid snapped a few pictures so he could figure out what each medication was for. He was able to slip out without being seen.

By the time he made it back to the apartment, the Thai food had already been delivered, and Jenna was sitting in her nook with a book and her food.

"Get your food," Jenna said, waving her chop sticks at him.

With a chuckle, he sat down at the island and pulled out his phone and began researching each medication he had found in William's apartment. Research page after research page, he looked for any ideas that would take care of the pest problem in the building. He watched the clock closely and gave himself just enough time for his research before his actual work would begin.

With forty minutes almost done, Sid headed for the stairwell and waited for William to head to the basement once more. Once he was in the clear, he slipped down to his floor and right into his apartment without being seen once again. Sid came prepared with gloves, as to not leave prints. A wicked smile crept across his face as he mixed around the medications, swapping out and replacing whatever either looked the same, or whatever would make sense. Messing with his medications would have to be the only step he could do at the moment, without risking getting caught. He didn't know what harm it would do, but he hoped it would be enough to at least get him out of this building.

Sid was able to slip out of William's

apartment unseen and arrive back to his own. Entering the apartment, Jenna looked up from her book. "Laundry?"

"Not quite dry, yet." He smiled sweetly at her. "I can head back down-"

"No, get your work done. How much longer on the dryer?" she said, placing her book on the pillow in front of her.

"Fifteen minutes." He made his way over to the table and shuffled through the mess of papers in front of him.

Jenna came up behind him and gave him a kiss on his shoulder. "Thank you for dinner."

Sid turned to her with a smile and placed a kiss on her forehead. "Anything for you."

Three days is all it would take...

CHAPTER TWENTY

"So, how did William pass away?" Jack said, leaning in towards Sid to slide him a cup of coffee.

Sid grabbed the cup and pulled it towards him. "I never got the complete story, due to the accident happening that following day. I know he was on house arrest, so he could not go far. They had an officer stationed right outside of the building because of the many complaints and the backlash that was received for allowing him to come back to his apartment. Many people complained because there were children in the complex, but officers, for once, were where they needed to be. When he attempted to leave at some point in time during the night, the officers made him return to his apartment."

"He attempted to leave during the night?" Jack asked.

"Said he needed to go to the hospital, but they just sent him back to his apartment. They opened an investigation into how the officers handled the situation. I believe they both were put on leave."

Jack shifted in his seat. "What do you think happened?"

Sid took a sip of his coffee. "I think he ended up having sugar issues. I read that having elevated blood sugars can cause stress on organs. He obviously had other medical issues, and they all caught up with him."

"Do you think what happened to the cops was appropriate?"

"If you are asking me if it is wrong that they got reprimanded for sending a sick man back to his apartment, instead of escorting him to the hospital, then no. Those officers were more than likely back out on the streets within a month or two. Officers should be held to a higher standard, but they still get away with a lot more than anyone will ever know."

"Let's rewind a bit and talk about the accident. What happened?" Jack said, scribbling into his notebook.

"That would be Verity's accident. She had just started walking and was getting around a lot," Sid said as he picked at his nails.

"So, what happened?" Jack said as he leaned in towards Sid.

Mason and Sid were carrying bags inside, just catching up on what life had served them over the past few days. Scarlett and Jenna had taken their weekly shopping trip and had bought more than they planned, like always. It was nice to have this little routine in their lives that involved people, other than just the two of them. Every Sunday, Mason and Scarlett would head to church. After church, Mason headed over to Sid's for some guy time. It was mostly beer and video games during the colder months, but when the weather was nice, they would go to the shooting range or out for golf. The girls, on the other hand, were always spending money shopping. Sometimes, they would just go for weekly groceries, but other days, like today, they went out and had fun, just the two of them, and Verity, of course.

"I should have never given her the new credit card," Mason said with a laugh as he balanced one side of a giant mirror they had taken out of Jenna's jeep.

"It would look great in the dining room!" Scarlett shouted as she set a wiggly Verity down beside her.

"And what do you wish to do with the pictures in the dining room?" Mason hollered back as he and Sid propped the mirror against the building.

Scarlett shrugged as Jenna giggled.

"And this, my dear," Sid said as he wrapped an arm around Jenna's shoulder, "is why we do not keep the credit cards out in the open."

Jenna scoffed. "I'm not the one with the shopping addiction! Who went to the store for a new printer and came home with a printer, a desktop computer, a gaming console, *and* all the little extras that you wanted for it?" Jenna fluttered her eyes at Sid. "And pray tell me, how much did you spend?"

Mason leaned over in a fit of laughter as Sid shrugged his shoulders and slinked away from Jenna.

Scarlett turned her attention away from the group and towards sirens that were becoming louder. "I wonder what is going on?"

Mason shrugged as he and Sid loaded their arms with bags from the back of Scarlett's van. The fun part of shopping was bringing everything inside. It was easier to park in front of the building on the street side, because the stairs were closer to the street than the parking area out back. They were always more cautious about Verity, now that she was getting around more. She was becoming a very independent little girl.

Sirens were getting louder now as Mason and Sid headed up the steps of the building. The strap on one of the reusable bags snapped, causing canned goods to fly down the steps. "We got it," Scarlett shouted out, grabbing a bag from the back of the van before heading over to the cans that Jenna had already begun to pick up. Jenna turned to place eyes on Verity as the sirens grew deafening. "I think she is trying to get her elephant," Jenna said, pointing to Verity, who was attempting to climb into the back of the van. "I got this; you go get her." Jenna's eyes turned towards picking up the two cans that remained. Sid, who had dropped his bags inside the doors, returned to help as well.

Before Scarlett could get out another word, a thundering crash echoed off the buildings. Ear-splitting screeching and the groans of metal twisting in unnatural angles followed. Jenna swung her head around to the street as Scarlett screamed out Verity's name. The path of destruction seen as taillights took off, away from the flashing lights that were approaching.

"Mason!" Scarlett shrilled, reaching out to a motionless Verity. Jenna dropped the bag, cans thudding as they hit the ground, as she rushed to Scarlett's side. She had scooped Verity into her arms.

Chaos erupted on the sidewalk in front of Sid. Mason's cries, Scarlett's wailing, the panic in Jenna's eyes, and the overwhelming number of emotions flooding around them. Sirens roared, breaks shrieked, and the overbearing flashing lights blinded anyone nearby. But it was the blood that stood out the most. The metallic smell that reminded Sid of a time long-forgotten. He watched as the blood seeped into the cracks of the sidewalk like a flowing river of rubies, a parent's greatest treasure, sliding right out of their fingertips.

»»»»»

"So, what exactly happened?" Jack asked.

"A woman who was driving under the influence of drugs and alcohol caused an accident a few blocks away from our apartment building. Something set her off, and when the police arrived to the first accident, she fled. She had hit several other cars on her rampage. Something caused her to swerve, though, near our apartment, and she hit the back end of Scarlett's vehicle and dragged her car across four others. Scarlett's vehicle slammed into Verity, who was standing just on the other side of it, attempting to climb in, and she was thrown to the pavement from the force," Sid said as he picked at his fingers.

"And the driver, she fled from that scene as well?"

Sid nodded. "She never even attempted to slow down. I don't believe she knew she had hurt someone, but she didn't even attempt to stop. A few officers stopped when they saw the damage, originally to make sure that everyone was okay, and then they saw Verity. Bystanders were already on the phones with emergency services at that point in time. Everything was happening so quickly but, yet, time seemed to stand still."

Jack leaned forward, "And Verity?"

Sid paused for a moment, biting the inside of his cheek. Running his fingers through his hair, he said, "They rushed her to the hospital, which, thankfully, was equipped for children. I guess that could be a plus to living in the city." Sid let out a heavy sigh. "You know, that lady was just going to walk. They arrested her that night. Because of cameras and whatever, they were able to track her back to her house. So, they found her and arrested her. She was out and home the next day!" Sid hit the table. "Chloe Baker got to go home, while Scarlett and Mason sat at the bedside of their only child while she fought for her life!" Sid took a low, deep breath. "I kept my nose out of it and let the law handle it, especially while Verity was in the hospital. We spent our days bouncing between the hospital, our jobs, and our home. I'm not a prayer person, by any means, but I went to bed every night, hoping that Verity would make it. Our friends, this was not something they deserved. They were good people."

Jack scribbled something in his notepad before looking up at Sid. "I'm sure Mason and Scarlett appreciated you and Jenna being there."

Sid agreed. "They were very appreciative of all that we were doing, even more so when I found out about that nurse." Sid scoffed. "It is bad enough to steal from the hospital you work at, but to steal medicine from your patients... Who steals pain medicine from a little girl?"

Jack turned his head to the side, "How did you find out that the nurse," Jack paused, glancing down at his paper, "Reagan, was stealing?"

"It wasn't easy, but I had walked in on her pocketing something one day. Reagan was smart about it, I will give her that, but she slipped up in front of the wrong person." Sid leaned back into his chair. "I followed her around the hospital, trying to make it seem not too obvious. She caught on, though, when we ran into one another outside of the hospital, and I called her out on it."

"How long were you following her?" Jack asked.

"I followed her for almost three weeks," Sid stated apathetically.

Jack nodded slowly as he scribbled some more into his notebook. "How long did it take you to catch her?"

Sid sat there for a moment, thinking back to the sequence of events. "Verity had been in the hospital five days at that point in time."

"And when you called Reagan out on it?"

Sid chuckled, "The newspaper said that the night of her suicide, she emailed her D.O.N. telling her what she had done. When Melanie, the D.O.N., received the email the following day, she noticed Reagan was a no call, no show. Police were called for a welfare check, originally, and they found her body in her apartment."

Jack shifted in his seat. "How did you kill Reagan?"

"Using the very drugs she had stolen from the hospital. Back when I had killed Danny, I learned about veins and how to inject into them. It was the same thing here. When I got into her apartment, she was already passed out from something. A few of the vials she had lying around were Ketamine, Fentanyl, Propofol, and

Morphine. I figured a mix of her stash would do the trick. I left no prints and finished the job. I also cranked the AC up, just in case it was a few days before they found her body."

"And Verity lasted…?"

"Two more days," Sid said with a sigh.

➤➤ ➤➤ ➤➤ ➤➤ ➤➤

Sid sat at the table shuffling through paperwork that had stacked up over the past couple of weeks. He glanced at a note, reminding him to return a call to Lucia. He honestly couldn't remember when she had called, but she wanted to speak with him. However, he was busy helping Mason and Scarlett. He made a mental note that he needed to call her this Saturday.

Jenna popped out from the bedroom, dressed and ready to go. "If you need to stay and work, stay and work. I'm just going to run them some food, and then I will be right back, okay?"

Sid walked over and kissed Jenna sweetly. "I promise that when you get back, I will be cleaned up and ready to go."

Jenna brushed her hand across his cheek. "We don't need to go tonight. I know you hate events like this."

Sid shook his head. "But you love them. I'm not a people person, no, but you have been looking forward to doing something other than this." He motioned to their messy apartment. They had been so busy with everything, they just hadn't had a time to clean like they normally would.

Jenna smiled widely at Sid and gave him a quick peck, but before she could reach the door, there was a light knock. Jenna opened the door to reveal a disheveled Mason. His eyes were puffy, and he stumbled into their apartment without glancing at either of them. Jenna and Sid looked between one another as Sid tried to analyze his surroundings. Mason's hair was wet, but it was not raining. Maybe he had come home for a shower and was just too tired to drive.

Mason dropped like an anchor onto their couch, burying his head into his hands.

"Mason?" Jenna said softly, approaching with caution.

"She's dead," Mason said dryly.

Jenna took in a sharp breath, as Sid tried to process what was just said. Sid looked up at Jenna, her eyes wide, with tears filling the corners.

"I came home for a shower! A stupid shower, and she died while I was gone!" Mason grabbed a throw pillow and stood while chucking it at the wall. "She's dead!" he screamed as he pulled his hair. Mason collapsed onto the floor, and Sid rushed to his side. He grabbed his friend and just held him there while he sobbed. Jenna sat with her back against the wall by the door, sobbing softly. Today, the world became a little darker.

"Verity's death was hard on everyone." Sid rocked back and forth in his chair. "I was so angry about the entire situation. I just snapped."

"And killed Chloe?" Jack inquired.

Sid nodded, "I went straight to her house, so, thankfully, she lived alone."

Jack nodded in return. "How did you kill Chloe?"

"It was very similar to the situation with Anthony. She took some medicine to help her relax and got in her car, like I told her to. She begged and pleaded, but I reminded her that there was a little girl who would never see her second birthday, lying on a metal slab, while she got to sleep in a nice warm bed. I told her if she got out of her car at all, I would kill her. She started her car, closed the garage door, and went to sleep. Honestly, it was a very nice way to go out, compared to what had happened to Verity. Chloe Baker could have, and should have, suffered a lot more than she did, so she should have counted herself lucky."

"Is this the point in time where Jenna began to ask questions?" Jack asked.

"Yes." Sid shifted in his seat. "She asked where I was and what I did. I told her I did what I needed to do. That is as far as the conversation went."

Jack nodded, standing from his chair. "You are doing great, Sid. You have really come a long way with everything. We will not have another session this week. Jenna is going to be visiting instead. You deserve to see her before we move on."

"Just in case I go manic again?"

"I want you to take a couple of days to prepare for what is going to come next."

Sid leaned onto the table, placing his head between his hands. "Lucia..." he sighed.

CHAPTER TWENTY ONE

Life continued to be chaotic for Sid and Jenna. Phone calls home became a very seldom event, not that it happened often before. Lucia pushed for Sid to call more, but between work and Verity's death, he was just too emotionally drained. Sid was pushing for a new position, which involved a lot more work than normal. More of Sid's files slowly made their way home, and Jenna began hinting that they needed a bigger place for an office and maybe an extra room or two. Sid continued to make promises to Lucia to call when they had time to say more than a few words, and he maintained in his stance that they would head home for at least one holiday. Lucia wasn't the only one who hounded them. Tammy, Charlie, and Aria all began to pressure Jenna and Sid to come home for a bit.

Finally, Sid caved and made plans with Jenna to surprise everyone by making a spontaneous trip in the middle of the week. He loaded up what files he would need to work out of the office and headed home with the intent to travel to Glenwood the following day and not return until the weekend. Because of the impromptu trip, Jenna was going to have to use a few sick days that had been slowly adding up. But, as so many times before, something would happen that would put a barrier in their way.

At 3:00am, Jenna received a phone call from the store manager. She was told someone had broken into the store, and they needed her to come in. Normally, she would not need to respond to an incident like this, but because the pharmacy was also impacted, she would need to come in. Jenna had no choice but to head in to work and assess the damage. Every single pill would have to be counted, including any prescriptions that had not yet been picked up. It was going to be a long day. When Sid woke up, he went looking for Jenna and, instead of finding her, he found a note telling him to call her. He tried not to worry as he waited for her to pick up the phone.

"What happened?" Sid said, trying to hide the nervousness in his voice.

"Everything is fine," Jenna said with a huff. "There was a break-in at the store, and they made it into the pharmacy and caused a lot of damage. I think all they ran off with were some narcotics, but we have to go through the inventory completely." She sighed. "I'm going to be stuck here all day."

Sid felt his chest lighten. "Well, if you need anything, you need to let me know. I can pick up lunch for everyone."

"What I want you to do," Jenna began, "is go see Lucia. I will fly in later tonight or tomorrow. But you need to go see her."

"I'm not going without you," Sid stated plainly. "I will just call the airline and reschedule both our flights."

Jenna chuckled on the other end of the phone. "I had a feeling you would say that." She let out a huff. "You really need to go see Lucia, but I know there is no use arguing with you. You won't listen to me."

Sid chuckled, "Stubbornness at its finest!"

"Move them to tomorrow. That way, I can concentrate on this, and we can fly out in the morning."

If Sid only knew the reason Jenna was pushing him to go, maybe he would have gone without her. He would have made it in time, but tomorrow was going to be too late.

Sid was not able to get a flight early in the morning. The first flight that was available was at three in the afternoon. The flight was quick, but the lay-over was longer than they originally expected. They were forced to have a six hour lay-over, due to a nice thunder storm passing above them. When they finally made it to

Glenwood, it was almost midnight, and the last thing Sid expected was to see Charlie standing in the driveway.

"Did you tell him we were coming?" Sid questioned.

"Yes, him and Aria knew we were coming." Jenna sat motionless in the passenger seat. "But... I..."

Sid pulled up right behind Charlie's truck, but something just wasn't right. Pain covered Charlie's face. Sid clamored out of the vehicle.

"Sid," Jenna said as she reached out for him, but it was too late.

"What is going on?" Sid asked.

Charlie's head lowered to the ground as Jenna approached Sid from behind. "I told her you were on your way..." he sighed heavily.

"Lucia? Don't be upset about that. I'm just glad I get to see her." Sid headed towards the house, oblivious to his surroundings.

Charlie grabbed his arm. "No, you don't understand."

A whimper came from Jenna.

Sid's attention turned to Jenna, who had tears filling her eyes as Charlie continued, "She didn't want anyone to tell you. She didn't want you to worry."

"Worry?" Sid ripped his arm from Charlie's grasp, turning his attention back to him. "What don't I know?" Fury filled his eyes.

"She fought so hard; you need to know that," Charlie said, placing a hand on his shoulder.

Just then, an ambulance pulled into the

driveway, and it finally clicked. Sid lunged towards the house, but Charlie wrapped his arms around him. "Lucia!" Sid screamed.

"You don't want to see her like this, Sid!" Charlie hollered back at him. The two men wrestled down to the grass as Sid attempted to claw his way to the house. Jenna had curled up into a ball, knees to her chest, in front of their rental, sobbing. "Sidney, stop!" Charlie yelled.

"No!" Sid screamed, agony piercing his every word. "Lucia... God, no!"

Aria stumbled out of the house from the commotion and found her way to Jenna. He could hear everyone around him, yet shrieking pierced his ears even louder. His shrieking. "Lucia! Let me go!" When Aria finally reached Jenna, Sid had finally stopped fighting Charlie and was weeping into the grass. "Mom..." Sid mumbled, his voice hoarse, defeated. For the first time in his life, grief swallowed him whole. He was not sure how long he laid there on the cold ground, his heart thumping so loudly, he prayed it would just stop. When Charlie helped him up, the ambulance was gone, and Jenna was already inside. Lucia never hurt anyone, she didn't deserve this. Heading inside, the house felt empty. Aria had made coffee, but he just stared into the cup as he listened to Charlie while he explained what happened.

"Two years ago, she got her official diagnosis. With her blood work being off and the lump they found, they worked as quickly as they could to gain control of the situation. She had surgery, and they

237

removed both of her breasts, even though only the left was affected. She went through radiation treatments, and within a few months, she was told she was in remission. Lucia hid it from all of us. No one knew except for Randy. She had no choice but to tell him because it was going to interfere with her job. So, she thought she was in the clear. Four months ago, she ended up in the hospital, as she was having trouble breathing. They found cancer in her lungs and surrounding areas. The cancer had spread, and this time, there was no surviving it. Lucia sat Aria and I down and told us. That was when I started to call, pushing you to come home. She said that if you wanted to come home, you would when you could. Lucia told me she needed to be the one to tell you, and that it couldn't be over the phone. Jenna knew Lucia was sick, but she didn't know the specifics."

Sid just sat there, staring at the cup of coffee in front of him. The sun had begun to rise, and the light was peeking through the curtains behind him, but it wasn't the same. It would never be the same. With Lucia gone, his life was just as dark and meek as the cold, blackened coffee before him. What was there left to say? He let life in the city get in the way of a person who mattered more, and there would be no way to undo it. There would be no goodbyes, just a bitter, empty house full of memories they had created together. Standing from the table, Sid stumbled away and headed straight to Lucia's room. It was empty but full at the same time.

Medical equipment spread across the room. The bed was a mess, blankets and pillows scattered. She died in here, right at the edge of his fingertips. He needed to be alone. For the first time since he was seven-years-old, he wore his grief on his sleeves and let it swallow him whole. Wrapping himself in a blanket that smelled like Lucia, he curled into a ball on her bed and cried himself to sleep, mourning what he had so selfishly taken for granted.

Three days would pass before he would eat or even speak to anyone. Jenna gave him his space and was there when he was ready. He cried on her shoulder, and she comforted him the best she could. One week after her passing, he finally was able to muster enough strength and started to pick up the house. He would find a letter waiting for him on the desk, with Lucia's writing on the envelope. He couldn't bear to read it, so he stuffed it in his bag for a later date. Two antagonizing weeks would go by after her death before her funeral would happen. The day of the funeral would change everyone's lives forever.

Sid voiced his pleasure in the funeral. It was a very beautiful service, Lucia would have been proud. Sid arranged for Lucia's casket to be carried and had family on one side, and close friends on the other. Charlie, Sid, and Carlos carried the casket on one side, while Mike-Andy's father, Marcus-Aria's father, and Randy-Lucia's boss carried it on the other side. Sid had opted for a closed casket, as well. Even though she was being buried in her favorite dress, he wanted to remember her before she was sick. He wanted to remember her bright eyes, her loving smile, and the way she lit up a room before she became sick. The entire town came out for her funeral. There were even people in attendance that he never thought he would come face to face with again.

Out on the sidewalk in front of the funeral home, six people stood in a circle for the first time in many years, almost like time had not passed at all. Jenna and Sid stood hand in hand, facing the old friends. To their left stood Aria and Charlie in the same manor, hand in hand. To their right were faces long forgotten, both different in how life had changed them. A blue and green-haired, bright eyed Rachel stood next to a rundown Andy, who now had to walk with a cane. The accident had really messed Andy up, but Sid had heard that he had been clean and sober ever since. It seems that, sometimes, good can come from the bad.

With the funeral and graveside service done, Sid and Jenna invited their friends back to the house. It would be the first time since Lucia's death that Sid would smile, but his smile would be short-lived.

Rachel could only stay a little over an hour, as she needed to catch her flight back home. She had a residency that she needed to get back to, because she reached for her dream. Soon, Rachel would be addressed as Dr. Wilson. Charlie and Aria were able to stay for a few hours. They needed to head to the bakery before heading home because Aria had a truck making a delivery, and they needed to put the items away. When they headed out, Jenna headed to the store, as they were running low on almost everything in the house. At least that was what she had said, but he had a feeling that she just didn't want to be around Andy. Ever since his impromptu visit in Trenmont City, she had been uneasy around even the mentioning of his name. With it being just the two of them, he hoped maybe he could get to the bottom of the issue and fix it. No matter what had happened, they were friends, right?

"I'm sorry about that," Sid said, motioning towards the door.

"It isn't her fault, you know." Andy picked up a pool stick off the wall and headed towards the table. "I can't believe how bad I hurt her."

"You talking about when you visited?" Sid questioned.

"I have no excuse for my actions, I know that. I know forgiveness may never come from those I have hurt, but I will continue to try to make up for everything." Andy leaned up against the table.

"Sounds like you got your head on your shoulders now." Sid returned next to Andy with a pool stick of his own.

Andy nodded. "I have a clearer head, that is for sure. I honestly didn't think you would speak to me after what happened that day. I was so ashamed of myself for hurting Jenna."

Sid stopped in his tracks and tried to process what Andy just said. He thought back to that day and remembered Jenna at the bottom of the stairs. But Scarlett said she slipped. Sid would need to get more information from Andy because, obviously, no one was telling him the truth. "I know you didn't mean it."

Andy chalked up his stick. "I needed money so bad, at least I thought I did." Andy scoffed and half threw the cube of chalk. "And then, accusing you of killing Logan... I was out of line."

"I never knew about the Logan situation. She never mentioned it to me." Getting him to talk was going to be harder than he thought. Sid walked around and racked up the balls. "You know, if you talk about it, we should be able to put it to rest. I can help you come up with a way to apologize to Jenna, see if we can work together. So, let's start at the beginning." Sid motioned for Andy to make his move on the table.

Andy took his turn as he began discussing what happened that day, how he had showed up, looking for money. Andy had been watching the apartment building and knew that Sid wasn't home. They took turns taking their shot as Sid continued to listen to Andy's words. Jenna refused him money right away, asked how he had found her again... again? Andy caught onto Sid's expression and answered his question without having to voice it. Andy had run into Jenna at her job and began stalking her. On more than one occasion, he had been inappropriate with her while outside of her work. So much so, that she threatened to call the cops if he didn't leave her alone.

Sid had never heard of that. Jenna never once mentioned it. He kept himself calm, even though deep down inside, he already wanted to strangle Andy. He needed to know everything. So Andy continued. When he finally made it into the apartment, Andy was upset that Jenna wouldn't help him. He was mad at the fact that Jenna lived a cozy little life with a murderer, while he sat on the streets eating scraps. Sid watched as Andy's demeanor changed with the mention of what happened next. Andy told Jenna that she should be with a real man, that he could show her what a real man was like and that maybe she would help him then. Jenna fought back, eventually caving, saying if Andy took his hands off of her, she would go get him some money. That must have been when she called Sid. Anger bubbled up from the pit of his stomach, but Sid kept his breathing even as he continued to listen to Andy.

Andy skipped over the dinner and went to when Jenna chased him down in the stairwell. Even though he had hurt her earlier in the evening, she was still attempting to save him. Andy described how he grabbed onto Jenna and shoved her to the stairs, before smacking her across the face and calling her a name that he couldn't remember. He just knew she began to cry while he ripped into her about her murderous fiancé.

Sid tried to tell himself to stay calm, but he could feel himself losing his grip. As Andy leaned across the table to take his shot, Sid let out a chuckle.

"What?" Andy asked.

"It is crazy that you knew." Sid spun his stick around in his hand.

"Knew what?" Andy lined up another shot.

"That I killed Logan." Sid placed his eyes on Andy, who stumbled a bit at his words.

Andy let out a nervous chuckle, turning towards Sid. "Nice one."

Sid motioned to the table, "Finish your turn." He waited and watched as Andy lined up his shot once more. "I am very protective over what is mine, and I have honestly killed for less."

Andy froze in place, still turned away from Sid.

"But I know a way you can fix this," Sid said, weighing the pool stick in his hands.

Andy turned slowly to meet Sid's dead stare. "How?" he said, swallowing the visible lump in his throat.

Without a second thought, Sid swung the pool stick, cracking Andy right against the skull. Andy stumbled to the side and, due to it being his injured side, he fell to the ground. Sid hovered over him, his chest heaving with each breath. "You put your hands on her and think that is okay?!" He swung the pool stick again, the loud crack echoing off of his skull.

"Stop!" Andy screamed.

"Like you stopped?!" He swung again... and again. Andy's screams turned into whimpers, as a blind rage consumed Sid. Andy didn't stand a chance. When the pool stick snapped, Sid dropped to his knees, grabbing Andy by his collar.

Andy's face was bloody and split open in several spots, he was almost unrecognizable. "Please..." Andy begged.

"Please?!" Sid roared, spittle flying off his lips. Sid raised the pool stick above his head and plunged it into Andy's abdomen. Pale eyes wide and glassy, Andy's head fell against the ground behind him. In his rage, Sid continued to stab him with the broken pool stick, the warm blood soaking into his clothes, becoming sticky and cold, the metallic smell gripping the air around him. It wasn't until he heard the car tires clattering against the gravel driveway that he realized what had just happened. He dropped the pool stick next to Andy's lifeless body and stumbled out of the garage and into the house. By the time he reached the front door, Jenna was headed across the lawn with bags in her hand.

Jenna froze at the sight of Sid in the doorway, covered in Andy's blood. The bags dropped to the ground as Jenna shrieked, "God, no!"

Sid stood there, watching as the world around him slowed down, Jenna dropping to her knees, crying out as he brought his hands up to eye level. He watched as the crimson liquid flowed down his arms like the river of tears that were falling from Jenna's eyes.

CHAPTER TWENTY TWO

"Andy's death, do you regret it?" Jack asked.

Sid shook his head slowly. "I do not regret it. I will never regret any of my kills. They each were deplorable and their actions unforgivable."

Jack shifted in his seat. "You always reference *their* actions and *their* consequences, but what about yours?"

"I am here, for a start. I have been told that I am clinically insane, whereas, I don't see it. I know that what I did, people do not agree with, but so many times I have watched the system fail those who it is meant to protect. I watched as innocents suffered, while evil continues to walk the streets. Politicians fight and argue over laws, and those who are meant to uphold them either do not know the laws or break the laws themselves. Our system is corrupt and crumbling at our fingertips. The only thing the people we elect can seem to do is argue over what to fix and, in return, they fix nothing. We continue to let our streets be overrun with those who do not deserve the light of day. We continue to fund the corruption around us, while the innocent most always suffer in silence." Sid paused, taking a breath. "If I could be the one change in the world that can make it better one piece at a time, why not do it?"

"Do you understand that what you did, it was wrong?" Jack leaned forward.

Sid huffed, "It isn't wrong, that is what you don't understand."

"But you killed people."

Sid's voice raised as he sat up and thrusted his finger into the table. "Who didn't deserve to be here!"

"And you deserve to be here?"

A moment passed between Sid and Jack as they stared at one another. "No," Sid said dryly. "I never thought I would live this long... let alone, fall in love. I do not deserve her, and I don't deserve the life I had." Sid turned his head away from Jack, his jaw shifting, as he thought about Jenna. "I don't understand it." Sid watched from the corner of his eye as Jack sat there in silence. "What?" he said as he turned his attention back to him.

"What don't you understand?"

"Why I, of all people, still live. If I am as bad as they believe me to be, why do I still live? I don't see myself as innocent, but I don't see myself as deplorable as they do. I helped people, the only way I knew how. Do I deserve to live? No, but for whatever fucked up reason, I am still here, so I will do what I can to make sure those around me are not hurt."

Jack scribbled into his notepad. "And Jenna, wasn't she hurt by your actions?"

"She forgives me, even though she doesn't understand why. She thanked me for taking care of Danny. Charlie felt the same way when we talked. He didn't understand, but he forgave me for what I did to Hud."

"Forgiveness does not excuse your transgressions, Sid."

"What I understand is that, in the eyes of those who have created, as well as break, the laws, I deserve to be locked up for the rest of my life, at least. So, lock me up. I didn't plea insanity, they said I should be here. I confessed to Jenna because she deserved to know the man she was with. She still continues to stand by me, even knowing what I have done. She doesn't believe me to be insane, she doesn't believe me to be a monster. I listen to her, because she shows me respect and doesn't let others influence her opinion of me. She told me I would need to tell the police, so I did. During every step, she was by my side."

"That was all it took for you to confess, was her asking you to?"

Sid nodded, "Yes."

Sid was lucky enough to have people who loved him. He stayed in the jail only over the weekend, and they bailed him out Monday morning. Everything around him, though, was falling apart. Jenna had returned to the city to handle taking a leave of absence from her job. Charlie and Aria opened their home to Sid, with a few stipulations. Sid couldn't blame them for being a little uneasy, but Charlie voiced that he couldn't let his brother sit behind bars. Aria was able to get Sid's bag from Lucia's house, with the help of an officer. That way, Sid would have some of his things while he waited for the trial to happen, if it did happen at all. Sid's lawyer was pushing for Sid to plead insanity, but Sid kept refusing. Sid wanted his day in front of people, he wanted his voice to be heard.

The first night at Charlie's house, Sid opened his bag to find Lucia's note. He placed it on the bedside table and stared at it every time it crossed his vision. He wanted to open it, but it was hard, knowing that if there were questions that arose from it, he would never have answers. By the morning, he would finally open it. Deep down, he wished he had read it before the funeral, and maybe, just maybe, he would have had a chance to live a life with Jenna...

My Sidney,
I honestly wish we could have talked face to face. If you have found this letter, that means I did not make it, and we never got a chance to talk about everything.

I knew I was going to die, but I wished that I could have seen your face one last time. I don't blame you for leaving Glenwood, and I understand why you had to leave. Trenmont City gave you and Jenna a chance at a fresh start, but your dark cloud followed you there.

I am so sorry, Sidney. I wish I could have helped you.

I know I am partly to blame. I should have stood up to Arthur, and I know, no matter what I say, I cannot take back what he put you through. My actions, as well as Arthur's, left you no choice but to do what you did.

I didn't see it at first, and I am sorry. I know what happened to Arthur wasn't an accident. It took me a long time to see it. You showed me all the signs that you had reached your breaking point, but I continued to put you through all of that mess. I promised to protect you, to give you a better life than what was handed to you, but I failed you.

I have sat back and watched as people have died around you, and I know I am to blame.

I am sorry that I couldn't help you. Please, for the sake of Jenna, please do not hurt anyone else.

Bury your sins and live the life you deserve to have with her.

You deserve to be happy. Don't let the horrible world around you make you question that.

I love you, and I am sorry.

She died believing she was to blame. Sid crumpled up the letter and threw it. He was so angry. He didn't do what he did because of her. How could she think that? Lucia was an innocent; she had no part in any of this. He did what he did to protect her. Why didn't she see that? One by one, Sid threw the contents of his bag around the room as he screamed out. He hated himself for not coming to her when she needed him, and he would never be able to fix what he broke. She was gone, and she left this world thinking she was the problem. No, she was not the problem, he was, and she would never know that.

> ≫ ≫ ≫ ≫ ≫

Sid sat in his room, staring at the walls. With his story on the record now, he had no idea where the sessions with Jack would go. Sid was found not guilty by reason of insanity. His lawyers were able to prove that the expansive abuse and mistreatment were factors in his actions. Even though his ideals and viewpoints on the world had not changed, what would happen to him now? He knew he would more than likely never see a world outside of this institution, but at least he would be able to see Jenna. During their last visit, he tried to get her to move on with her life, but she refused, like always. He didn't want to continue to drag her down, but she wanted to be by his side. Charlie was coming to visit tomorrow with Jenna. It was going to be the first time he could see Charlie since his breakdown several months ago, so he was looking forward to it.

As he sat on his bed, he saw a shadow from the corner of his eye, and he knew right away what was happening. He just hoped that whatever transpired would not take away his visitation tomorrow.

"Well, well, well. If it isn't the monster himself," Tyler said, his tone harsh, as always.

"Good evening," Sid said, hoping to keep their interaction on the positive side.

"You will never guess what I did before work today, but try," Tyler said.

Sid sighed.

"Go on! Guess!" Tyler said, more forcefully this time.

"You got food?" Sid asked, his voice flat.

"I got coffee and chatted with a beautiful woman. We got talking, and I think we really hit it off."

"Happy for you," Sid said, dryly.

"She is in town just for today and tomorrow... Visiting, so she says."

Sid's hands balled up into fists, gripping the edge of the bed. Jenna would be in town, staying at a local hotel before her visit. How could he have known she was in town? There is no way, unless Jack let it slip. Tyler just wanted to get under Sid's skin.

"Had a very nice guy with her, said it was her brother-in-law." Tyler continued, "Gave her my number so she could get a hold of me before she leaves."

Sid closed his eyes and concentrated on

his breathing. He needed to remain calm. Lashing out at Tyler would not go over well. The only person in this facility who knew that Sid called Charlie his brother and referred to him as such in conversations, was Jack. There was no way that Tyler knew that without an outside source. Sid realized that he truly had to have run into Jenna.

"I told you I was going to show her what a real man is like," Tyler hissed through his teeth.

Sid rose from his bed and lunged towards the door. "Why don't you open this door and say that to my face? Fucking coward."

Tyler threw his head back in laughter that twisted Sid's stomach. "I cannot wait to feel her satin skin and her soft lips."

"Go to Hell, you fucking pervert! You touch her, and I will kill you!" Sid screamed.

Just then, a door slammed, and he knew they were no longer alone. "What is going on, Tyler?"

"This one is having a hard time settling down. He may need some help tonight," Tyler said, turning towards the voice down the hall.

"Fuck you, asshole!" Sid screamed. He knew deep down, Tyler got what he wanted, but Sid would not go down without a fight.

"Let me grab some help, Tyler," shouted the voice.

"And some medication! Let's put him down for the night," Tyler shouted back as the sound of the door echoed off the walls of the bare hallway.

"You try to touch me, and I will break your arm," Sid said through gritted teeth, seething, knowing that this just might take away his visitation with Jenna and Charlie. "This is the only way you can prove you're a man, by attacking me and going after someone who wouldn't give you the time of day. She would never pay attention to someone like you. She knows what kind of man you truly are."

"I can show you what kind of man I truly am. I can make you cower in a corner. You will learn to respect me, murderous freak."

Sid hit the door standing between him and Tyler, just as the echo of the doors sounded once more, followed by the thudding of footsteps, as they headed down towards Sid's room. If he was going down, it would not be without a fight tonight. Tyler was stealing everything from him, just over one incident. He was tired of Tyler's shit. That attitude of his, he was long overdue for a reality check.

When the door opened, Tyler was the first to rush into the room, and Sid hauled off with a hook, straight to his jaw. He continued to fight head on with Tyler as others rushed around him and attempted to pull him off. Tyler made one wrong move, placing his hand in front of Sid's face. Sid bit with all his force onto the side of Tyler's hand, and Tyler screamed out in agony. The yelling that was passed around the room was muffled by the sounds of the chaos that ensued. Sid fought with everything in him to escape their grasps, but his actions were futile. He felt the sharp piercing of multiple needles and the burning sensation of the familiar liquids being forced into his muscles. The warm sensation began rushing over him, his muscles became weighty under the sedation that was just enforced upon him. His eyes grew heavy and fluttered closed as the surrounding noises faded.

He wasn't sure how long he had been comatose, but it couldn't have been too long, as there was still someone in his room. With all his might, he forced his eyes open to see an irate Tyler standing in his room, his eyes wild, and an eerie feeling rushed over Sid. They were alone in the room, and the door was closed. Sid attempted to rise from the bed, but with one small push from Tyler, he crashed back down. "You just don't learn, do you? This is my house, and you continue to disrespect me!" Tyler's voice was hushed, but Sid could hear brutality slicing through his words. Sid was still under the influence of the medication. He would not be able to fight back, and Tyler knew it. The unknown of what was to come gripped him with a fear straight to his core. Would he beat him, torture him?

"Don't... don't do..." Sid forced out.

"Do what? You have what is coming to you and so much more," Tyler hissed through his teeth.

Sid was yanked off the bed, and his body fell to the floor with a thump. He continued to try to get up, but his muscles were still too weak from the sedative. He had just enough strength to raise his head, to meet Tyler's gaze, and see what was coming next for him. "I'm going to show you a real man," Tyler said through gritted teeth as Sid watched his pants drop to the floor.

CHAPTER
TWENTY THREE

Sid did not move when the morning nurse made her rounds. She gave him a once over and moved on, not questioning his silence. He rarely talked, so they would not question his silence. He was not going to talk with anyone, especially Jack. He opened up about Tyler to him, and it didn't do anything. Speaking up about what happened would get him nowhere. No one would believe him, anyways. The pain pierced him with every movement, reminding him what had happened. It was a memory that seared into his soul that he would never forget, let alone forgive. He did not leave his room for breakfast, but when lunch rolled around, a familiar face appeared in the doorway.

"Sid," Jack called out.

Sid continued to stare at his ceiling, refusing to acknowledge his presence.

With a sigh, Jack stepped into his room. "I'm not sure what happened last night, but Jenna and Charlie are here. Do you still wish to see them?"

Sid shot up from his bed but winced once the pain hit him. "They are here?"

Jack nodded. "Yes, but do you need to see the nurse?"

Sid shook his head. "No, I just want to see them."

Within thirty minutes, he was face to face and in a long-awaited embrace with his angel. He gripped her tightly, thankful she was safe from the antics surrounding him. Breathing in deeply, the smell of home rushed through him, honey and coconut and happiness. Charlie, clearing his voice, brought him back to the stark reality where they stood. Her scent would not last forever, but he would enjoy it as long as he could.

"Hello, brother," Sid said as he left his embrace with Jenna.

"Sid," Charlie said with open arms. Without a moment of hesitation, the men grasped one another for a quick hug. If only Charlie knew how much it meant for him to be here.

With the pleasantries out the of way, they all sat down and began talking about life. Jenna had moved back to Glenwood to be closer to her mother, who had fallen ill. Charlie and Aria had been helping to find a place and the help that Jenna would need to keep her mother home. Even though Tammy and Jenna had their rough moments, Jenna would do anything for her mother, and it was comforting to know that Jenna was no longer alone every night. Charlie talked about how the business had expanded, and Aria was now offering catering services. The bakery had originally expanded to include a little coffee shop, but she quickly had to upgrade to a bigger place, as more people began asking if she offered packages that included food. They hired a cook and expanded to where they were currently at. Charlie hadn't done much with his father's business, other than build it back to its former glory. They concentrated more on Aria's expansion.

Jenna pointed out that Sid was very quiet, but he just shrugged her off. He stated he was tired and didn't have much to share, as exciting stuff didn't normally happen here. Jenna stepped out to use the restroom, while Charlie and Sid made jokes and reminisced about old times. When she returned, though, her attitude had dramatically changed.

"What happened last night?" Her arms were crossed over her chest, her eyes hard.

"What do you mean?" Sid asked, attempting to brush it off.

"They sedated you, why?" Jenna was short with her words and obviously angry.

"Can we not discuss this now?" Sid said, turning away from her.

"Was it that Tyler dick?"

Sid let out a huff, realizing she wasn't going to let it go.

"It was, wasn't it?" she questioned once

again. She approached from behind and lifted his shirt before he could protest, exposing bruises he received the night before. "Oh, my god..."

Sid swatted her hand away, standing. He moved to the other side of the room to escape her wrath that was going to follow.

"Who is Tyler?" Charlie chimed in.

"He is a nurse who works here, who has been giving Sid a hard time for a long time, and no one is doing anything about it!" Jenna's voice was loud enough to cause Jack to come in. She shifted on her heels faster than Sid could stand and came face to face, wagging her finger in Jack's face. "You!? You were supposed to take care of the situation! And now, he's covered in bruises and was drugged!"

"What happened, Sid?" Jack asked.

"Nothing," Sid said dryly, his attention facing away from them, out the window.

"I cannot help you if you don't tell me what is going on," Jack said.

Sid continued to stand at the edge of the room, his arms crossed over his chest.

"Out, both of you. I want to talk to him alone," Jenna said, and from her tone, she wasn't giving them a choice.

"Charlie, if you want to follow me, let's give them a moment," Jack said as he opened the door.

Once the door closed behind them, all that was left was the echo of Jenna's foot as it tapped against the concrete floor. "What happened?"

Sid turned to Jenna, displeasure plastered across her face. With a sigh, he sat down at the table and told Jenna exactly what happened. He started with the rumor that she had run into him at the coffee shop, which turned out to be true, and ended with the rape.

Jenna rose from the table, without saying another word, and left the room. He knew Jenna wasn't mad at him, but he never expected for her not to return. The only thought that crossed his mind was that they escorted her out. Jenna had a hot temper, and when she was pushed repeatedly, she would snap. He knew that Jenna would have told someone what had happened. He half expected for Jack to show up, but he didn't.

Leaving the family room, Sid was escorted to the medical wing, so someone had to have found out. Hours passed, and multiple people attempted to get Sid to consent to an exam, but he continued to refuse. By dinner, they gave up. Whispers floated around, stating they would try again tomorrow, before they allowed him to hit the showers. They needed him to allow the examination. He knew if he wanted anything to come from this, he would need to consent, but couldn't they just give him the night? He just needed some space, a chance to wrap his head around everything.

That night, they left him in the medical wing, and an eerie stillness descended upon his surroundings. The number of people that checked on him decreased by the hour until there had been no one for quite some time. He was the only patient in the medical wing, and the nurse had been gone for over an hour. At the first clamor of noise, Sid's senses went on high alert. He laid there in the bed, eyes closed, hoping they would pass by him. The last thing he expected was a familiar voice to speak up.

"Get up, now!" came a whisper from a voice across the room from him. His eyes opened, and he couldn't believe what was happening. "What are you staring at? Get up!" Her voice was harsh.

"What are you..." Sid began to say.

"You're telling me, that you are just going to sit by and let him get away with what he did to you? Tell me it isn't eating away at you, and I will leave right now, without you." Sid's eyes widened. "You only have roughly twenty seconds to make up your mind."

"Why would you risk everything for me?" Sid questioned, sitting up from the mattress. The figure came face to face with him, grabbing him and forcing him to his feet. "Me and you, we are woven from the same thread. Deep down, we are the same. You have said that hundreds of times, and if I were in your shoes, I would not be able to live with going through something like that and not be able to take care of it." She brushed off his shirt. "Let's get you out of here and take care of that bastard together." Her blue eyes burned into him, and he took a deep breath, taking in his surroundings - honey and coconut.

With eyes hard as steel, a wicked smile crossed Sid's lips as he looked down at his blonde-haired, now fallen, angel. "Let's go, my love."

Darkness in front of them, a sunrise slowly creeping on the horizon behind, Jenna and Sid sped away from Brookhaven, knowing that, once they saw he was gone, they wouldn't have long. Fingers interlaced and hearts racing, they headed into the unknown. Tyler would face death face to face with a fallen angel at his side.

TO BE CONTINUED...

Want to know where Sid and
Jenna end up?

Visit:

www.michellemartinez.net

To be kept up to date with
announcements and giveaways.

Part 2 of Hellion comes out in
2021.

Michelle Martinez is a Western New York native with a love of books; a mother to three young boys who were her inspiration to branch out and try something new. Writing had always been a hobby for Michelle. It was never something she thought she could make a living with. At the beginning of the COVID-19 pandemic, Michelle was home with a newborn while attempting to help her older boys distance learn. After staying at home with her boys for several months, Michelle wanted to find a way to work from home. After playing around with old writings,she realized she had something valuable to share with the world and has turned to writing full time.

Since turning her passion into a profession, Michelle Martinez has written prolifically and is constantly exploring new themes, genres, and ideas. It's incredibly hard work, but she's never happier than when she sits down at their desk putting the opening words to a new book or story on paper.

Hellion is Michelle's first published work as an Indie author.

Visit www.michellemartinez.net to stay in contact with Michelle and follow her journey.

Made in the USA
Middletown, DE
20 January 2021